AT BUTTON'S

AT BUTTON'S

Garry Wills

ANDREWS AND McMEEL, INC.
A Universal Press Syndicate Company
KANSAS CITY

Library of Congress Cataloging in Publication Data

Wills, Garry, 1934-
   At Button's.

   I. Title.
PZ4.W74175At   [PS3573.I45658]   813'.5'4   78-27763
ISBN O-8362-6108-9

To my favorite two Lydias.
both, like Lydia of Philippi,
dealers in purple.

CONTENTS

1

In the Foyer:
New York, 1977

i

HE CAME IN A SEQUENCE OF HESITATIONS AND DIPS breathtaking. Even the sweater he dangled by one arm danced. Ed Jones, the reading room guard, jumped up from his half-slumber and said, "No dogs allowed here"—as if the fellow could have brought a dog past the outside doorman and up the lone publicity of the New York Library's stairs. Ed looked over at Gregory's desk, hoping the research librarian had not heard him. But Gregory Skipwith winked.

Since he was caught anyway, Ed came over to the raised desk and whispered, "That guy's *got* to be part brother. You whites can't move like that." The two looked out over the reading room, its inhabitants dwarfed by high space luminous with dust. It amazed Skipwith that so many people came to plead for books from that electric board so clearly meant to cow and discourage them.

"Your class is about assembled," Ed said with a survey of the room. "There's the Fondler over there, still kneading his pud-

3

ding under the table. And the Nodder. Looks like everyone's here except the Babe." They called her the Babe because young boys kept inventing reasons to walk past her, and the other side of her reading table was always jammed with men who held their books low. The Babe wore nothing but a flimsy shirt above her jeans. Outside, on Forty-second Street, she would hardly attract a glance. The repressive literary hush made her light up, here, like a dim bulb in a basement. "I wonder what she reads?" Ed continued. "Whatever it is, it's good for the health."

Gregory had wondered too; but found no excuse to check her book titles. He didn't want to join the line of sightseeing boys, and she never came to the reference shelves for his help. Skipwith had taken this job to avoid dealing with people, to live with the deaths he had to puzzle through. But the very isolation he sought made him curious about others as he had never been when "studying people" as a business. He did keep track of his regulars, like a teacher tending class. By his second month on the job, Ed had taken to greeting him: "Mornin', Teach."

Like most teachers, he had his pets. There was the retired fireman writing a history of New York's fire departments in a script so large that a simple sentence filled most of a page. He left with a bulky manuscript every night; but a typewriter would sizzle it down to two pages or so, if a typewriter ever got a chance at it. Most manuscripts written here would never see print.

There was the natty businessman who came in every day and spent his lunch hour writing and crossing off lines of verse; one or two unblotted lines were his daily prize—Skipwith wondered if these stray phrases ever got connected somewhere else. He had come to think of his "pupils" as such fragments— disconnected phrases he could not assemble outside this cave of words.

One could watch the Mumbler all day. She checked out the

same book, a history of the American West, opened it, and never turned a page. Staring at the blur of print, she took up again her long quarrel with the world or herself. Her tones changed—patient, explaining, accusatory, accused, haughty, pleading—but no one around her could catch a single word; and very few sat close enough to try. One man used her music as a kind of soothing background. He always chose a chair with its back to her—that was just the right distance for the hum, which shut out other (less steady) distractions.

Ed had drifted back to his post, and Gregory glanced that way when he heard some truly heroic throat clearing. The Babe was bouncing in. Though she rarely looked at anyone else, today was different. After putting in her book order at the desk, she strolled down the aisle, humming a bit, and rumpled the Mumbler's frizzy hair. This had no effect, of course. One could no more frizz that ultimately frizzed hair than break into the Mumbler's busy, inert world. The Babe shrugged, nodded a few times in agreement with the Nodder, and slumped into her chair.

Ed came over again, and Gregory said, "The Babe must be flipping her lid."

"Why not? She flips everything else." Gregory laughed and got some angry stares. Even Ralston tsk-tsked him from his far desk.

Ralston was the only regular Gregory knew by name. They had met when Ralston, whose very clothes were quiet, raised his whisper brusquely and asked, "Who the hell moved Groves?"—each monosyllable spaced, neatly ictused as if with a rubber hammer.

"Oh, sorry, I did. I wanted it near me for browsing on dull afternoons."

"You mean *some* afternoons are exciting in here?" Ralston had relaxed at once when he heard that Skipwith browsed in Groves. "Are you a musician?" he asked.

"No, just an opera nut."

"Verdi, I hope?"

"No, Wagner." Ralston stiffened again, a little.

They bumped into each other during lunch hour in the park behind the library. Ralston, whose clothes folded round him layer on layer like feathers, was feeding the pigeons. Gregory sat down to eat his own sandwich; they exchanged names.

After that, they met once or twice a week for lunch in the park, mainly talking opera from two distant planets. Samuel Ralston, who grew up with opera and was rather bored by it, had been converted the first time he saw Licia Albanese as Mimi. He followed her around the world, from that time, excusing her late coquettings, looking for a successor to his affections (Judith Blegen the current contender). Skipwith, a Flagstad and Nilsson man, wondered how a bright fellow like Ralston could mistake flirting for singing. They traded amiable insults as they waded through the bright dust and shuffle of New York's pigeons. They had waved hello at the Met a couple of times—no more, since their tastes were so different. Skipwith still didn't know what Ralston did for a living, or why he came in so often (though only for brief sessions) to look up and copy out passages from books.

After the mock tsk-tsking, Ralston took his books to the desk and asked if Gregory was having lunch in the park.

"Yes, when my replacement comes."

"Meet you there."

By the time Skipwith got the lunch bag from his locker, Ralston had his briefcase open. His notes were mixed in with peanuts for the pigeons.

"The Babe is getting exuberant. At this rate, she'll kiss the Fondler or put a match to the fireman's coat."

"You keep a close watch on your flock, don't you? What's my nickname in your free puppet show?"

"I couldn't give you a name. You gave me your name—beat me to it—before I could name you."

"Close call. What would it have been—dirty old man?"

"No, neat young man. I might have called you Neat. Even Spiffy. Have you ever worn spats?"

"No, but I've wished to."

"That's it, then. Spats."

Ralston looked suddenly uncomfortable. "I hope you won't call me that before others. We'll be taken for mobsters."

"Don't worry. I'm trying to break myself of the name-giving habit. If I don't, I'll have to give up the job."

"Why?"

"It's bad for the soul to be naming the animals like Adam. I make up their stories, I'm giving them each a secret life of my own imagining. It gives me an odd feeling of mastery over them."

"What's wrong with that? Writers do it all the time."

"I do it because I can't write. I came here thinking I could put down a story in my odd moments at that desk, but it was my own story and it drained me. So I've taken to stealing bits of life from those dim people in there. God knows they have little enough to give. I shouldn't be sucking at them like some Dracula of Forty-second Street."

"Well, it's better than being an out-and-out voyeur."

"I don't think so. Voyeurs must be overstocked, if anything, with fantasies and imagined acts. They hardly need more of that. I think they want to touch down again with reality, just look at some intimate thing for its own sake; get out of make-believe, and believe in some plain old fact. That's how I think of Warhol's bloody soup cans. He's spying on their reality. They totally lack fantasy; so they feed the fantasist."

"Maybe. But I hope you're wrong about voyeurs."

"Why?"

"I'm one."

"You? Why, you never even look around at others in the reading room."

"Oh no, that would be too easy. You can stare at them all day, and they won't notice or care. I have to hunt people who are suspicious, in parks and subways and stores. I see how long I can observe them without their observing me."

"Why?"

"Oh, my analyst has theories. But I prefer my own."

"Which is?"

"I have to deal all day with sycophants and those trying to please me. It's refreshing to watch people who are not watching my every move to anticipate it and ingratiate themselves."

"What are you, a millionaire?"

"Well, a son of one. I have nothing to do with the family business. I thought I could escape that world by helping run the family foundation. I'm the talent scout. I look for actors, painters, musicians who need help."

"What brings you here so often?"

"Mainly checking up on the grant petitions, doing my homework to see if they've done theirs. It takes me to the actors' club, the Richard Rodgers library—and, of course, here."

"Interesting work."

"No, rather sad. I have to turn down the sweetest people and give a hand to the perfectest turds. I know very well I am probably destroying humanity when I reward talent."

"There you are. You write other people's stories too. You have the power to give the happy ending, the blow of fate, the ironic twist. You play Fairy Godfather to all those Cinderellas. I couldn't stand that." He saw he had been carried away, and mumbled, "Sorry, not that I . . ."

"That's all right. It's my own feeling half the time. But you have to admit, I spy on people to show I have *no* power, for the joy of *knowing* I have no power over them."

"It must keep your analyst busy."

"Oh, I gave him up. I wanted to put myself in his power, but he was trying to ingratiate, too. I tried another, under a pseudonym, so he wouldn't know what kind of money he was dealing with. But he sensed it. I don't know how their vision tests on the unconscious, but they have a positive radar for the checking account."

"Well, now that you've blown your cover with me, I suppose I'll have to avoid you or you'll think I'm trying to ingratiate . . ."

"Oh, I didn't mean . . ."

"Forget it. I'm less in a mood to ingratiate than to demand. It just occurred to me you must be rolling in free tickets to the Met, and you never offered me one."

The poised Ralston looked sheepish for the first time since Skipwith had known him: "I wanted to, but I was afraid you would consider it condescending. As if you were a charity case."

Skipwith laughed a silly high laugh that startled the pigeons. "You run a huge charity as your family's tax dodge, and you're afraid you'll be suspected of charity. I think you better find another analyst."

Ralston was relaxed again. "And you think you are sapping people's souls because you've given them nicknames. When I find one, I'll recommend him to you. You don't know what real power is. Every time I turn down people who, whatever their limits, are more talented than I am, I think this might be another Licia Albanese not yet come into her power."

"What do you mean? She was born with her power—the power to be prettily awkward. You must be a pushover for any girl artfully gawky."

"But that steels me against Wagnerian ladies with their foghorns."

"Sirens, maybe; not horns. Power with little vibrato is like space music. Your white voices sound unreal, like a boy's— Judith Blegen, for God's sake. But a clean *big* voice like Helen Traubel's comes like some laser from another planet."

Their planets had drifted apart again, rotating in friendly antagonism. They had negotiated that tricky moment each, for his own reason, feared—the moment when another person finds out who he is. Ralston offered him a ticket to the next night's opera. *"Otello.* That should satisfy both of us. I'll meet you there with my lover."

"Good. I'd like that."

So, Skipwith reflected, putting his apple back in the locker. He was not afraid to let me know he is a homosexual. Odd, that only the homosexuals have the courage of their affections these days. If Ralston were bringing a woman, he would have said my wife or mistress or date or mate or lady friend or girl or secretary or—something. But not lover. That is a bit of gay bravado. Rather nice.

The afternoon in the reading room began slowly, as usual. Heads were dropping as people napped off the sluggish effect of their lunches. The Conspiracy Nut came over to Skipwith for advice. She was a shy little woman in her forties who was studying plots ancient and modern, weaving them all together. Skipwith had given her the address of a friend who specialized in Elizabethan conspiracies. Late in the day a whispered quarrel broke out between two men, both snake-spitting and rattling their papers. One claimed the other had taken his seat. He appealed to the Nodder, sitting nearby—Skipwith could see it coming. The Nodder vigorously agreed with anything the first man said. Then he just as vigorously gave his assent to the second man. Each said, almost together, "Stop agreeing with *him,"* and both withdrew to nurse their joint grievance at this indiscriminate approver, who went back to approving of his book.

The Babe continued to be restless, though she did not once look Skipwith's way. She never did. But just at five, when the Fondler regularly buttoned his fly to go home, she walked straight up to him, hesitated, and then went back to her books. Grabbing her sweater, she walked past Skipwith, her eyes on the floor, but said with a fluttery voice, "Fooled you, didn't I?"

ii

It surprised Skipwith at first, but then he thought, of course! Ralston would have a dumb blond. He was gorgeous, all tight clothes and V-neck silk blouse. Ralston lived in a sheath of layers, grey on grey. He had wingtip shoes and wingtip hair, everything wrapped neatly over everything else, a flexile mummy. The Blond was tan everywhere one could see—which was saying a good deal. Skipwith felt like giving Ralston a wink, but played it safe.

"Meet Shelly Johnston." Shelly's handshake was incredibly sincere.

They gave in their tickets and milled toward the Met's stairway, heading for Ralston's box. Conversation was slow. Skipwith made with some all-occasions art talk. "These breastbone stairs always remind me of some Georgia O'Keeffe scene."

Ralston nodded: "A bleached pelvis, perhaps."

Shelly looked puzzled; then offered, tentatively, "Are we the maggots in the pelvis?"

Ralston answered without enthusiasm: "Very good, Shelly."

After the first act, Skipwith and Ralston agreed that a weak Iago unstrings all the tension of *Otello*. "One thing always surprised me about Shakespeare's Othello. He makes Iago very proper around his leader, but lets him talk bawdy to Ophelia."

Shelly tried again: "I think one should always talk a lot about sex before doing it with anyone. To find out if you are both thinking the same way."

"You know what this means, Gregory?" Ralston said portentously.

"No."

"That those magazine 'playmates' probably *do* say all those things printed in the margins of their pictures."

Skipwith looked up with surprise, and saw Ralston's eyes twinkling with complicity.

Soon after, Shelly withdrew, saying, "I must go repair myself."

"He hardly looks in disrepair," Skipwith said.

"No, he is very ornamental."

"You Tarzan, he Jane?"

"One hardly wants ornaments that talk back. Imagine it—talking furniture." He smiled, then shrugged. "He's extraordinarily—clean."

"A gem in the rough."

"That's the trouble. When you polish them, you lose them. But you polish them simply by having them."

The Iago improved just as his part was diminishing. Operas cannot get along with rough gems.

Afterward they went to the Brasserie for onion soup. Shelly seemed to know half the people there. He even looked like some of them. They were bantering over sopranos when Ralston ducked his head down over the soup. "Oh-oh, here comes a pest." Skipwith didn't look immediately, but said, "I'll scout, if you tell me what he looks like."

"Not he. It's someone who's been after me for a grant. She has bangs that go all around her head."

After a glance: "It's safe. She went to a counter stool. What's the matter with her project?"

"She did a master's at Columbia, now she wants to turn it into a book—the sociology of prostitution. You'd be surprised how many requests like that I get. It allows college kids to do a little slumming for their degree. It used to be men who asked. Now it's mainly women. They think they are going to be the Margaret Meads of Lexington Avenue."

"Well, at least it keeps them on the street."

"You mean off," said Shelly. "The saying is off."

Ralston shrugged and Skipwith said "Oh, right."

"Actually, this one is not as bad as most. The liberation types want to free the whores. They're not content to observe."

"Not so much Margaret Mead as Spartacus?"

"Right. Women's liberation plays the oddest changes on old reform themes. Redeeming the fallen sisters was a project of the temperance and suffrage ladies, too."

"But this one doesn't want to redeem?"

"No, just understand them. She majored in understanding, I think. The first thing she told me was that she would *understand* if I turned her down. She bullies you with understanding."

"So, did you turn her down?"

"Not yet. I don't *want* to be understood by her."

"Duck again. She's steering toward the ladies' room."

"Why, Mr. Ralston. Isn't this a coincidence? I just came off my midnight shift."

"You do your work in shifts?"

"Yes, prostitutes are creatures of habit. I've never dealt with people who are more punctual. May I join you for a minute?"

"Of course." After the introductions—her name was Marcia Roquist—she went for her soup while they cleared a space for her at the table.

Skipwith rose and held her chair. "How quaint," she said. "There are so many disappearing customs to record in our culture."

"I hear you are half-worlding it, Miss Roquist."

"What? Oh yes, but the demimonde has its own haut-monde styles and codes. There's a midnight decorum among them, a set of things that 'are not done' even by people who do everything. It takes a long time to see what rules they live by, since they have never been codified."

"And you are working out this *etiquette noire*?"

"Trying to. That will depend on Mr. Ralston here."

"Yes, we are still studying your request."

"I have many new leads since I wrote that. Could I submit another one to you?"

"I think we have enough to go on."

"That means you are going to accept, right?"

"What makes you think so?"

"I'm sure you would entertain further evidence if you were leaning toward rejection, wouldn't you?" Neat, Skipwith thought. He wondered if she managed her whores as neatly.

"I think we fear you might be romanticizing a rather sordid world."

"Well, it's another world. You must observe it without preconceptions, as we would a strange tribe in Australia. You have to understand people from within. They see *themselves* as civilized. Indeed, they maintain a civilization of their own against tremendous odds. All things considered, they may be the most civilized New Yorkers!"

Skipwith was beginning to understand Ralston's reluctance to issue this grant. "Australian tribes did not choose to be isolated or primitive. Your half-world lives defiantly in a center of world civilization."

"Most of the girls have had no more choice than a Pygmy in Africa. Natural selection pushes them out onto the street."

"But what of the pimps?"

"They are the most fascinating of all. They have elaborate unspoken treaties worked out among themselves. They do not raid each other's girls. Though they jockey and compete for turf, one withdraws gracefully when the other has established some minimal jurisdiction."

"How do they communicate these exquisite rules to each other?"

"In sign languages of many sorts—principally their dress. A pimp is pure symbol. He flies semaphore flags all over his person and his car. Some think he dresses to cow his girls. Actually, he dresses for his peers. They are competitors; but they are also a club. When it is said a pimp does no work but drive around all night, you know you are talking to a person who does not understand any culture but his own. It is their *job* to be out there. Their work is being *seen*. You don't say a flag is doing nothing when it is up on its pole all day."

"What is the hold a pimp has on his girl?"

"Fear and admiration. It's a carom shot, actually. The girls are impressed because the other pimps are impressed. That's why they see their pimps as protectors rather than exploiters. Each one protects them from indiscriminate exploitation by ten other guys."

"Do you get mistaken for a prostitute out on the avenue at midnight?"

"Of course not."

"Why? You are young and pretty."

"Whores have their flags, too, and I'm not wearing any. My jeans are enough to disqualify me."

"They look better to me than most of those slit skirts with the mesh stockings showing."

"You've never had a whore, have you?"

"How did you know?"

"The sleaze is part of the lure. Johns have to have glamour, but of the kind that doesn't intimidate. It is a *nostalgie de la boue* in men who like their mud to come with sequins. Besides, the *girls* need it. They know the glamour is contrived, but it gives them some sense of control over their 'careers.' An actress knows how all the lights and stage illusions work; she does not feel the emotions she is feigning on the stage. But she feels the excitement of feigning excitement, and of generating it. The best actresses in the world wouldn't go onstage with the lighting system on the blink. Besides, all whores are trying to catch the pimp's eye as an actress angles for the director's attention. Their money comes from the johns, but danger and romance and twisted love all come from the pimps. Pimps are the social stabilizers in every way. Take them off the street and it really would be a jungle. The pimp keeps order without violence. He does it all with color and signals—like a traffic light."

"I never knew there could be such force in a velvet hat."

"Those who first looked at our tribe wouldn't believe that huge trucks obey tiny red lights, either."

"True enough."

Shelly was beginning to yawn, so Ralston bustled to leave. "We'll let you know," he told Miss Roquist.

"Have a drink?" Skipwith asked her. Neither Ralston nor Shelly drank.

"Okay, a glass of white wine."

She kept up the rather breathless description of her research. "I did a biography of ten women for my dissertation, divided according to different geographical origin. I have kept up with them and added five more since. I need about thirty to make a book; but unless I get some grant money soon, I'll have to go back to Toledo and beg dough from my father."

"Don't the girls' stories get depressingly similar after a while?"

"But *pattern* is what makes a *culture*. If each story were different there would not be anything to study."

"You got me there."

"Besides, there are some exceptions. I'm meeting one at two o'clock. You can say hello, but then you have to let me talk to her alone. I haven't been able to get her to a taping session; but she's softening."

"What makes her so special?"

"She's a free-lancer. No pimp, no regular turf. They don't normally last a week, but she is known to have friends among the cops and pimps, and she works for free."

"Why?"

"Who knows? A kook. That's why I want to study her. Even the exception can help one understand the rule, *if* one understands the exception."

"Something tells me you will."

"Tell me something about you."

"Research librarian in the main reading room on Forty-second Street."

"A lifelong career?"

"Maybe. If they'll let me stay."

"Is it enough to support a wife on?"

"No. No wife, anymore."

"You prefer Mr. Ralston's type?"

"No, just his taste in the type."

"Then what's the matter?" She said it with a terrible menace of understanding.

He panicked. "I must be going."

"Oh, stay for Sybil. She's already a minute or two late. That shows she's not a pro." Skipwith had already risen when she started waving her arm and said, "Over here."

Skipwith smiled and sat back down when he saw the girl on the stairs. It was the Babe.

iii

"Hello, Mr. Librarian. Is your name Marion?"

"No, Gregory."

"Mine's Sybil—Sybil Collins."

"An intriguing mix."

"Mind if I have a real drink?" She had looked at theirs. "I sometimes think New York women will just trickle down a subway grill someday when the chablis takes over their whole system. Give me gin any day. It cooks off faster." She placed her order for a double Beefeater on the rocks. "Has teacher here been tattling on me to my other teacher? You know what this interview is all about?"

"Yes."

"Are you her research assistant?"

"No, we just met. I had no idea she was talking about you."

"How could you? You didn't know my name. Or did you?"

"No."

"You must have given me one, though."

"I'm afraid so," he admitted weakly.

"What is it?"

"The Babe."

"Not very imaginative. I expected it to be dirty. Well, it's as good as Sybil, I guess."

"What takes you off the street this early?"

Marcia frowned at him for asking the questions, and doing it so bluntly.

"Hasn't she told you? I come and go as I please, just trying out new situations. I collect kooks. I've got a peach of a one for you tonight," she said to Marcia, who took out her notebook.

"I look forward to hearing it, but couldn't we go put it on a tape?"

"No, thanks. Besides, I want Gregory to hear what his pupil is up to at night."

"All right. Talk slow. I don't take shorthand."

"Of course not. That's what we liberated women got liberated from, right?"

Marcia, with her nose in her notebook, said vehemently, "Right."

"Well, as you know, I cruise looking for the different customer. I have ways of knowing. Tonight I got a kind of professor, put a little hook in him and trolled him for blocks, playing him out and pulling him in. He was bashful, but I said I would not put up with anything normal and that seemed to relax him. We went to his library in a brownstone, where he cleaned off a desk and asked me to lie on it naked. 'Nope, I've done the black Mass before.' He was shocked when I said this. 'Oh no,' he said, 'I just want to write on you.' 'Not with a knife, I hope?' 'Oh no.' He had a permanent blush, so I couldn't tell what really embarrassed him as I undressed and he did too. Then he brought a yellow pad over and placed it on my mount and started jabbing at it with a pen, writing every dirty word he could think of. He scribbled and jabbed till the paper was a tangle of lines over lines, hardly anything yellow still peeking through. Then he cried 'Now,' tore off the sheet, and got off his knees. He had an erection at last, and he strapped the pen on his penis with two rubber bands. I could see he was practiced at this move, he did it quick so the erection would not fade. Then he wrote five or six words on the second sheet of the pad, guiding his own penis, but putting my hand around it and the pen as he wrote in a shaky big child's script. Then he quickly got dressed. 'What is it?' I asked him. 'Poetry. One line at a time. I am writing a poem from the creative force of the universe itself.' 'Is that all?' I asked him. 'Yes, it takes it out of one to serve as the conduit of universal energy.' He tried to pay me, but I turned him down, and he toddled off to sleep, sweet thing."

Marcia asked a few questions, then excused herself. She had to go to the ladies' room and write down all her impressions of Sybil's bearing and involvement in this episode. She was already wondering where she could look in the literature for a parallel to this fetish.

Skipwith, studying Sybil, said, "I've heard of writer's block before, but that beats all. Was there any truth to it?"

"Not a word."

"Why string her along?"

"She needs a break from all her dreary schoolwork. She wants kooks. I supply her with kooks."

"You don't collect them for yourself, you're just her agent?"

"She's the Duveen of kookifacts, and nothing is too good for my patron."

"Actually, your story reminded me of someone."

"The executive type who comes in and works on his one line a day?"

"You've noticed. I thought you kept to yourself, like Ralston."

"Oh, Ralston sees what's going on around him. He's just not open about it, like you."

"I think you could give our lady anthropologist in the bathroom a lesson or two in observing."

"Oh no, I'm giving her an advanced course in bullshit."

iv

Next morning, when Sybil came into the library, she did not look at Skipwith. He tried to catch her eye, but gave up after an hour or two. She left without saying a word. He had already looked in the phone book but did not find her name there. He toyed with the idea of asking Marcia how to call her, and then realized how absurd that was. If he wanted to see her, why not say so in the library? But some taboo kept him from doing that. Teacher should not play with his pupils.

He had fallen into a habit of reading himself to sleep with a mystery story in his one-room apartment, but that night he was restless. He turned on Home Box Office, saw a disaster movie wipe out half the character actors still at work in Hollywood, and went for a walk. He found himself, near midnight, walking up Lexington past the Waldorf. "Lonely?" the high-heeled black girls with red wigs lilted from doorways. He looked for a pimp, to read his semaphores, but saw none. He looked for Marcia, too. In the Brasserie, he sat at the counter where he could watch the door. He was not sure which of the two he hoped would come in, Sybil or Marcia. But then Marcia came in, and he was sure. It was Sybil.

Marcia saw him, joined him, ordered soup. While she chatted about this night's crop of whores, Skipwith kept glancing at the door. When the soup came, he could no longer see Marcia's eyes—her smooth cap of hair dangled out as she bent over. He reached, tried to loop the front bangs up, but they fell down again. "If I can't do anything about my hair, certainly *you* can't. It makes me look like a mushroom, I know, but if I let it grow, it looks like I'm wearing a lampshade."

"Your hair is fine. But you shouldn't let it hide your eyes." Her eyes seemed to peek over the lower part of her face, as over a wall: quizzical, animated. Wide child's eyes peeking into the circus tent of life. He wondered when it would stop being a circus for her.

After a while, she said quietly, "She's not coming, you know."

"What?"

"You keep looking at the door. Sybil told me she will not be back for a while."

"Why?"

"Who knows? She comes and goes. Among other things, that reduces the danger for her."

"Don't you mind the danger?"

"I'm pretty safe now. Enough girls know me to stick up for me. It was scary at the start, though."

"What makes Sybil risk it?"

"Well, she tells me several stories."

"So I noticed."

"Yeah. Was she pulling my leg last night?"

"I think so."

"Oh. Well, the best version I can put together of her life is that she wanted to work in one of her father's factories, under an assumed name. Her father said that would deprive someone of a job really needed. He tried to send her abroad to college. She told him that might deprive someone of an *education* really needed. She tells me she works the street for free so she won't deprive some deserving whore of her fee."

"You believe that?"

"I don't know. Some of it. Some of the time. I wish I knew. Maybe I will, if I keep at her. Want to help me?"

"Spy on her, you mean?"

"Of course not. She tells me stories of her own free will. What's wrong with trying to understand them?"

"That's the trouble with understanding. It always means intruding. I tried to understand a woman once. It got her killed."

"Now you're pulling my leg."

"No, I wouldn't do that."

"Tell me about the woman."

"No, I wouldn't do that."

"Was she your wife?"

"No, and don't ask what she was."

"That's no fair. You mentioned her, you got me curious."

"See what I mean? The simplest explanation of anything tangles you in the lives of others."

"That's what gives life its interest."

"It emptied life of interest in my case. Curiosity kills—and not just cats. I've taken the pledge."

"You seem curious about Sybil."

"I guess I am—and that makes me glad she won't be coming. I can't get involved with the people I see in the library. Ralston excepted, of course."

"Why of course?"

"Ralston's safe."

"You mean the way homosexuals are considered safe escorts for rich wives whose husbands can't stand the opera?"

"Good Lord, no. I mean he's another foyer man."

"A what?"

"It's the way I think of certain people who know they have to keep life at a distance if they are going to keep together any life at all. It comes from a poem by Hilaire Belloc."

"A short poem?"

"A sonnet." He recited it mechanically, without inflection; no smile—not even at the satiric line on the English:

> "The world's a stage. The trifling entrance fee
> Is paid (by proxy) to the registrar.
> The orchestra is very loud and free
> But plays no music in particular.
> They do not print a programme that I know.
> The cast is large. There isn't any plot.
> The acting of the piece is far below
> The very worst of modernistic rot.
> The only part about it I enjoy
> Is what was called in English the 'foyay.'
> There will I stand apart awhile and toy
> With thought, and set my cigarette alight;
> And then—without returning to the play—
> On with my coat and out into the night."

"I think that's rather horrible."

"No, it's a protection from the horrors."

"Besides, you're wrong about Mr. Ralston. He is intensely curious and involved. He made the rounds of my subjects with me one night. He was full of questions and compassion."

"He was just checking out your grant."

"No, I could tell he was interested in the girls for their own sake."

"Oh, that's right. He is a subdivision all to himself in our group of foyer men. He likes to go out among the people like a king in disguise, so no one will treat him well for his money's sake. He's a foyer voyeur. I'll bet you a buck he asked you not to tell any of the girls who he is or what he does."

She silently opened her purse and gave him a dollar.

"He renounces his power over people by going out and watching them. Only he never really escapes that power. If he had found a whore moving gracefully, he would probably have given her a dancing grant. Another Cinderella for his collection. Someday he'll have to give up people watching, too. Not even watch the play. Just stand in the foyer."

"Is that what you do?"

"Not yet. Not entirely. I still sneak a glance at the play. I watch some people from my library desk. I feel tempted to name them, give them stories. But the temptation gets weaker all the time."

"Come out and talk with my subjects. I'll bet I could get you interested again."

He looked at her a long time, her lift of eyebrows in anticipation. "You might. You're a carrier. You'll infect a lot of people before the disease burns out in you."

"What 'disease'? I study whores, I don't imitate them."

"No, a worse disease than that. Curiosity."

"I just want to understand others."

"That's the disease's worst degree. Understanding destroys."

"But you can't get through life without some interests."

"I used to think that. I thought there were safe interests, antiseptic, prophylactic. I thought I had found the perfect interest for preserving balance—love for an author who lived and wrote nothing but praise of balance."

"What author?"

"Joseph Addison."

"Addison-and-Steel Addison?"

"Yes, that's the way he comes linked to us in our school days. But saying Addison and Steele is saying ice and fire. I wanted only the icy part of the combination. A preservative, not a consuming fire."

"And even Addison didn't preserve you?"

"No, my interest in him ended my life."

"But you're still alive."

"Fooled you there."

v

As the weeks went by, Sybil came into the library less frequently. But now she said a polite hello and goodbye to Skipwith, and he replied politely. He had fought down the first tremor of interest in her. He went to the opera with Ralston and Shelly, and read his mystery stories. His own little foyer on life was quiet again.

Then, one morning, Marcia came to his desk and asked how she could get some Addison to read.

"Oh no, I thought I told you what he can do."

"I'll risk him. You should have seen the pimp I had to cope with last night. He thought I was trying to take his girl away from him. Addison will be child's play next to him."

"That's what I thought, once. If you're determined, go back out into the card room and get the number for his *Spectator* papers."

She spent all that day reading *Spectators*.

As she was leaving, Skipwith asked her how she could make her rounds after reading all day.

"It's the holiday weekend. Most of the girls are off visiting their children."

"They all have children?"

"What do you think brought them to the big city? Teenage pregnancy in a small town. The prudes keep us in prostitutes. The supply would dry up if small-town America ever got tolerant."

Tuesday, she was back at Skipwith's desk, carrying *Cato*. "Could I buy you lunch?"

"I brought my own. You can join me in the park; but Ralston's coming today. He may think you are trying to bully him on the grant."

"Oh, I got the grant all right."

"Then come eat half my sandwich."

"No, I'll go out and buy one. I live on a hamburger diet now, like my subjects."

"Gastronomical empathy?"

"Something like that."

. "I told you understanding others could kill you."

Out in the park, Marcia insisted they move away from the pigeons. But the pigeons knew Ralston too well. He dragged a scruff of them behind, as in an invisible net, and she had to surrender to their presence.

"I asked you out to pick your brain on Addison."

"Sounds painful."

"No, but Addison can't be as painless as you described him to me. Look at that passionate play, *Cato*."

"Yes, look at it. The eighteenth century heard him declaim 'Give me liberty or give me death' and thought he was expressing a preference for the former. Only those who knew him well realized that his disposition lay toward the latter. Whigs and Tories both claimed his play, and he gladly gave it to everyone though he was the Whig appointee. He took out the one directly political reference in the play."

"Is that what people really think of Addison now?"

"Those of us who read him."

"Are there many who do?"

"There used to be fifty that I knew of. I couldn't say now. There was a club of Addisonians, maintained at fifty members; but it dissolved three years ago in some scandal or other."

"Scandal around Addison?"

"Around some of the Addisonians. I hear there was an attempt last year to revive the club."

"Did it succeed?"

"I don't know. I only hear about it at all from a friend who asked that I make him a member."

"Can you do that?"

"Not under normal circumstances. You have to be in some

way a professional Addisonian. But this friend knows a little about everything and a lot about the Elizabethan period. They let him in to show they did not hold a grudge against me."

"Because of the scandal? You were mixed up in it, then."

"I died in it. Let's talk of something more cheerful. I haven't read a page of Addison in three years. My new anodyne is Nero Wolfe."

"What's your Elizabethan friend's name?"

"Wingate. But be glad you'll never meet him. What's in the Met's next season, Samuel?" Marcia crumbled her hamburger bun for the pigeons and went away. For two months she did not return to the library. Once or twice Skipwith saw her in the Brasserie and heard more about her whores.

vi

Early in July Marcia was sitting with a whore in the coffee room of the Summit Hotel. That shiny-suited bit of Miami architecture seemed at home in the swelter of a New York summer. The girls' tempers were snapping in the heat, and Marcia was having her recurrent doubt that she could finish her marathon of interviews. The names and faces of the girls had begun to blur now; the separate biographies were hard to keep separate. The little kick of danger no longer relieved the boredom. She got up at 11:30, arranged a time for taping this new girl, and started up Forty-ninth Street toward Park. She would call it an early evening, catch a cab home.

She was halfway up the dark block when she felt a hand on her wrist. She turned with fear, fumbling for the whistle she carried in her purse. But the little wino beside her kept one hand pinned. She tried to scratch him, but his head ducked around, he caught the other hand and held them both down beside her. They were face to face, his eyes near her chin. Even in her panic she was marginally curious that she smelt no wine on him. Later she wondered why she had not screamed. Maybe that was it.

"I hear you're interested in Addison."

"What?"

"I'm Ben Wingate. Have you heard of me?"

"Gregory's friend?"

"Right."

No wonder she first sensed him as a wino. He looked like a man not entirely down, but getting there. She wondered how two men as different as Wingate and Skipwith could ever have been friends.

"Are you looking for Gregory? We might find him at the Brasserie around the corner." She had worked him out onto Park Avenue. Papers blew past them, and kamikaze taxis dove under the Pan Am Building. She wanted to get him back among lights and people.

"No, I've been looking for you. Let's go back to the Summit, I don't want Gregory to see us together." He steered her to the bar, and ordered a double Scotch. She had reached her coffee limit, and had nothing.

"What's all this about?" She was still shaken, and her voice had the gulpy quality that is meant as bluster and comes out funk.

"I need your help. I want Skipwith to be at Button's next month."

"Be where?"

"That's what the Addisonians call their group—At Button's."

"After Addison's favorite coffee house." It was not a question, but an answer. She wanted him to know she could think straight though her voice still shook.

"See, you *are* interested in Addison."

"If you want Gregory to go somewhere, why don't you just ask him. You're his friend. I hardly know him."

"No one knows him anymore. Even I don't. That is one

reason he should go."

"Samuel Ralston knows him. He would be the one to ask Gregory, if anyone should."

"He already turned me down. I heard about you from him."

"You still haven't told me why you can't ask him yourself."

"Because he owes me a favor."

"All the more reason."

"No. I don't know if the favor would extend to this. The request might look too trivial to come under the heading of Favor with a capital F. Besides, if he did come for that reason, he would no longer owe me a favor, would he?"

"So you can't ask for a favor *because* you've got one coming to you."

"Exactly." He sounded like an approving teacher. That irritated her. But when she bristled, he went on the attack.

"For one who has been out on the streets for a while, you were awfully easy to take back there."

"Why didn't you just call my name then, instead of grabbing me?" His talk of "taking" reminded her that she had not got around, yet, to the deep mad she owed him.

"I did it to see if you were that easy. You should get off the streets. You're a baby."

Now the mad was fully there, satisfying: "What do you know about it? I know every regular girl out there and have met each one's pimp at least once." She was exaggerating in her anger, but not much. "I've never been attacked, except by a rude stranger who doesn't know the streets I do, yet has the gall to instruct me in them."

"Not me, sister. You're clearly uninstructible. So far. You've got your toe in a pond and you think it's the ocean."

"I'm not your sister, thank God. And I know the world I move in. I know its rules. In fact, I've written the rules."

"It's got no rules, just traps."

"It's got an elaborate hierarchy, turf treaty procedures, developed symbolism, structures of . . ."

"Crap." He said it matter-of-factly. "You interview these kids—eighteen, twenty-two—about their nasty daddies raping them at thirteen. Have you found out where they go from here, how long they live after their twenties, *how* they live *if* they live, and where?"

"No. How would I trace them when they go off the street?"

"Exactly. They go off the edge of the world. They go down—not to the bottom; where there is no bottom. The funny thing is they see others going down and they think they never will. They even deny their world has an edge.

"Ralston described your project to me. You think hundreds of the brighter whores have not thought up all that junk, and used it to deny their reality, the way they are being shunted to the edge? You describe these 'natives' forced onto turf they 'civilize.' It's not so complicated. Dumb girl, bright girl, guys leer at her and she gets the idea she's sitting on a gold mine, she's got the mother lode between her legs, just dig it out. It doesn't take long for them to find the mineshaft is really a black hole in space—they get sucked down their own cunt and disappear."

He spoke with a weary bitterness that took her breath away. It did not occur to her to argue back. He was not arguing with her. He was telling her. His quiet words had such weight they crumbled the whole structure of her project (which had been teetering in recent months). Now she knew why Gregory and this man were friends. Another foyer man. She could not argue with him, and would not yield to him. She looked for a way to change the subject.

"How can I help you take Gregory to some meeting?"

"Say you want to meet some Addisonians. Not join the club, just meet a few who are in town for the thing."

"He would just write me an introduction to the ones I wanted to see."

"No, I think he'll want to get you out of town and interested in a new subject."

"Why?"

"I convinced Ralston you were not only writing crap, but dangerous crap—dangerous to you."

"You mean he's going to recall my grant? What right have you to sabotage my work even before you meet me or see what I've done?"

"I don't think they recall grants. You can write your crap if you want. Just let Gregory think he is rescuing you from a fate worse than death by a change of scene and occupation."

"That's silly. It won't happen. Gregory takes pride in not getting tangled up in others' problems."

"Yeah, he's learning. But do you think that kind of isolation is healthy?"

"Do you?"

"I asked you first."

"No."

"Maybe this will cure him—meeting old friends in New Orleans, introducing you to men and ideas in an interesting place."

She realized he was not making the idea pleasant for Gregory but for her. "What's in it for you?" she said in her best clinical interviewer manner.

"I live and work in New Orleans now. I need a little help from him—something I could not ask him to make a special trip for. Believe me, it is not a big thing, it will take no time or effort on his part, but it will mean a lot to my future." He was not pleading. Just admitting his stake in the matter. He jumped from motive to motive as he considered this person or that—help, healing, selfishness, he kept all the balls in the air for an hour or so, and Marcia left feeling an urgent mission to take Skipwith to New Orleans in early September.

She reached him on the phone at his desk, and invited him to lunch—real lunch this time, her treat, to ask a favor. She would need a martini to make her act go smoothly, and he might give in more readily in surroundings more intimate than pigeon marbling. It was, she thought foolishly, their first "date." Skipwith told her not to get too fancy; he was wearing the shabbier of his two suits. She wavered: "Let's make it tonight then. You can change." That way she would have more time to prepare her pitch—and more time to persuade him. "Mercurio's by the Museum of Modern Art?"

"Sure. Meet you there."

"Seven?"

"On the dot."

And he was. After they were seated he said, "You're wearing your mushroom cap low again."

She looked up, not knowing how to start. Her eyes were uncertain—energetic still, but moving behind gauzes.

"I need some advice. I think my research is coming to a dead end, and I don't feel as safe as I once did out on the streets."

"I'm glad to hear that."

"If you don't think I'm moving in on your own field, I'd like to do a book on Addison."

"Do you have a new angle on him?"

"I think so. His use of ancient coins as more than archeological evidence, as an indicator of a culture's genius. You know: by your heroes you shall be known? Ruskin was only picking up Addison's work a century later when he wrote *Aratra Pentelici*."

"Yeah, but Ruskin stuck to Greek coins, Addison to Roman."

"And Ruskin either didn't know about his predecessor, or he chose not to acknowledge him."

"That sounds interesting—and, thank God, a good deal

tamer than structuralist roamings of the meat line. I'm afraid I don't know that side of Addison very well. I read the *Dialogues* just once, long ago."

"But you know all the members of At Button's."

He looked at her intensely, focusing. Had he mentioned the club's name?

"I thought you could introduce me to some of them at their next meeting."

"I don't even know there's to be a next meeting."

"There is. Next month in New Orleans."

"How do you know that?" His voice had gone up. He looked mad or scared or both, which scared her.

"A friend in the English Department at Columbia told me."

"Is he a member of the club?"

"No."

"What's his name?" She had been prepared for these questions, but not for the ferocity of their asking.

"*Her* name. It's Laura Schieff." She doubted he would check that, but Laura had agreed to back her story just in case.

"This makes no sense. I have vacation time coming, but I certainly don't want to spend it in New Orleans in early September. If the Addisonians are going there, they've lost their civilized judgment. You might as well hold it in one of Shelly's baths here. The Mississippi boils then. You don't want to go there. I'll get you the names of Addison art critics. Ron Paulsen would know who they are."

"But I'd like to see New Orleans. Heat doesn't affect me."

"It does me. You couldn't attend the meeting anyway. I don't even know if I could. I gave up my membership. As a matter of fact, my friend who became a member lives in New Orleans. I could get him to introduce you to the members most interested in Addison's aesthetics."

She sat there, silent, for a while. "Oh shit, this isn't going to work. And after all my rehearsing. I had you argued out of

every objection this afternoon. Stay dead! Screw your friend!"
She was mad now, and getting up to go.

"Wait a minute. How am I screwing you?"

"Not me. Ben Wingate."

He slumped back in his chair and said, in a low voice, "You
know Ben?"

"I do now. But apparently you don't. He has to scheme to get
a favor out of you."

"He schemes to go to the bathroom."

"Well, I still think there must be something wrong with you
if an old friend has to go through a mere acquaintance to get at
you."

"Please sit down. You're not a mere acquaintance—and he's
not a mere friend. When and how did he give you this silly
idea?"

"Here, in New York."

"Is he still here?"

"Yes."

"Where?"

"The Summit Hotel."

"Your stalking ground."

"Yes."

"Where you used to stalk, he stalked you. Stay here. I'll call
him."

He went out, was gone a good twenty minutes, while Marcia
had a second martini for the first time in her life, trying to
decide whether to stay or go.

"Let's order," Skipwith said when he returned. "He will join
us."

"What did he say?"

"You really want to know?"

"Yes."

"He said he thought you'd bungle it."

"Then why the hell did he ask me?" Skipwith looked sharply
at her. Martinis had swept the gauze from her eyes.

"Knowing him, I presume he asked to make you bungle."

"What sense does that make?"

"He thinks I'll go now to save you embarrassment. We're being used, my friend. And if Wingate stays around, you'd better get used to being used."

"Let's leave then."

"I did that three years ago. He'll find us when he wants us."

"You don't talk much like a friend."

"Oh, I like him well enough. I'm just afraid of him."

"Does he—have something on you?"

He laughed. "No, this is not the movies."

"He said you owed him something."

"Oh, that. He saved my life. Not much of a gift, it turns out."

"Stop talking like that. You and your foyer man pose. I suppose he's one of them, too?"

That made him stop in mid-drink, and cock his head at a new angle. "He's cut his ties, all right. He doesn't care. And it's true he doesn't want to see the show. But he still wants to get behind the scenes, monkey with those sandbags that shift scenes and bean comedians. He's indifferent, but he's an activist at indifference, if there can be such a thing."

"You know?" she said, almost in a whisper. "He looked so mousy, sitting in that bar, kind of bloodshot and all. But everything that should make him look pitiful gave him a kind of menace."

"Your observation has been improving, out on the street." She gave a little squeal as a grip closed on her right wrist. "Hello, Addisonian." Wingate slipped into the chair beside hers. Skipwith was up and wringing Wingate's hand with both of his, in obvious pleasure at seeing him. It was the first sign of affection Marcia had observed in him, and she thought it odd after his comments about Wingate.

Wingate ordered a double Scotch, and they started eating again.

"What's the game, Wingate? How many cards are you showing at this stage?"

"How many have I ever hid from you?"

"I've wondered about that—but none that I know of. Of
course, then we were accomplices. How come you planted so
many cards on this lady, instead of coming straight to me?
You'll never guess what a cover story she invented for you."

"The coins?" Marcia interjected. "They're a good thing,
don't you think? I might even do them."

"There you are," Wingate shot his sleeves in a "no cards"
gesture: "Just a midwife of the muses. Dedicate your book to
me, it's all the reward I ask. As for getting you back at Button's,
many of the members have asked me to do that. They are
distressed that you broke with them, and feel you somehow
blame them for what happened."

"That's nonsense. It has nothing to do with them."

"I know that, but they're doing the old minuet of misunderstandings: they think *you* blame *them* for blaming *you* for
making their little game blow up in their faces. So they have to
prove they don't blame you to make sure that you are not
blaming them." He nudged Marcia: "Follow that?"

"Yeah."

"I must be slipping."

"You've told me what others want, Ben. What do you want?"

"Straight to the point, eh? Okay. I have a little deal in the
works with Roger Slatkin, and I have to show him I'm a scholar
as well as a businessman."

"No problem. I'll send him a letter claiming you are the
greatest thing since Erasmus."

"No help."

"It'll have to be."

"I saved your life."

"You can have it back. I'd give you that, but not my time—
not thirty years with the memories I have been fighting these
three years."

This exchange had been slow, each man calculating rapidly but speaking with long pauses. They had forgotten Marcia. Each was weighing what he would risk, how much he could afford to wound. Wingate broke the tension first, rose with a whistling pucker of his lips, patted Skipwith on the shoulder, said, "It was worth a try," and left.

Skipwith and Marcia finished eating with few words. He put her in a cab, and she said simply, "I'm sorry."

viii

"No I'm not sorry!" The words popped in his desk phone, and turned a few heads near his desk in the reading room.

"I thought about it all night. I still think it damn little to do for a friend. Don't think of embarrassing me. I wouldn't go with you anyway. But *you* should go."

"Wait a minute. Let me explain."

Her end was silent. But the reading room had begun to buzz with curiosity. "Let's have dinner again."

"Oh no, not that."

"Then come to lunch—just here in the park." Pause. "All right?"

"All right." Skipwith heard a little insect-clapping to his left as he put down the phone. He tried not to look. But when he did, after others had gone back to their books, Sybil was smiling at him.

In the park, he went straight through the little speech he had been rehearsing since she called. "What you don't know, but Wingate does—that's why he tried to work through you—is that I quit a job three years ago to make a break with all my past, and especially with the At Button's part of it. I came to the library in an effort to stay sane. That meant being alone, avoiding certain thoughts, hammering out certain explanations. I tried to write down what had happened to me, as a way of controlling it. That didn't work. The theory of catharsis must be wrong—you don't flush things out, you just print them deeper." He spoke pedantically, as if discussing some case other than his own. "They say amnesia is a form of psychic self-preservation. I wish I could cultivate amnesia. I certainly won't cultivate memory by going back."

Marcia felt some weird distance between his melodramatic assertions and his dry manner. "Did you have a run-in with members of that club?"

"Please don't press me."

"Was Wingate involved in these horrors you claim?"

"He helped me through them."

"Then why would he invite you back into them? His effort could help make you overcome whatever it is that haunts you."

"Kill the dragon by throwing myself down its maw, is that it? Give it indigestion?"

"Well, you don't seem to be very successful at forgetting things up here. How would it be different down there?"

"I can't have more dealings with Wingate."

"But you looked happy to see him last night."

"I like him well enough. Well enough to become like him."

"Is that so bad?"

"There's worse, I admit. I found that out from him."

"What is all this hocus-pocus? Are you going to live the rest of your life mystifying others and pitying yourself?"

He got up abruptly and walked toward the library. Turned just as abruptly, grabbed her arm so tight she had to bite her lip to keep from whimpering, and dragged her off toward Fifth Avenue.

"You asked for it." In a savage voice, not looking at others, bumping into people, forcing irate men to jump around these two linked people half-running, he poured out the first stages of his story. It took blocks for Marcia to work her arm free, slow his walk, calm him till he sat in a little "park" on Fifty-third—a dent in the wall with a mini-waterfall at the dent's far end. She tried to slow him with questions, but he brushed them aside.

He rattled out his improbable tale, knowing too well how unbelievable he was making it sound—though it explained too much for Marcia to doubt a word of it. After an hour, he was up and pacing again, moving toward Central Park as she tagged along and tried to reassemble the first part of the story. She suggested he call the library, explain his absence. He shook his head no. "Get it over with." His hair was wet and he shivered a little in the hot sun. Marcia felt like an intruder now, and asked no questions. She tried to stop him from telling more. But he insisted. He told it over again, but not in sequence. He went back for lost details. He told it all.

2

At Button's:
Cambridge, 1974

i

IT WAS THE KIND OF LETHARGY THAT EXCITED SKIPWITH: A
muzziness with edge. The candlelight wove shadows around
the library. Their club's host for the evening was a friend of
Anthony Newman, who had just begun their after-dinner treat,
a performance of Bach's Italian Concerto. Light hit Skipwith's
brandy, through the snifter, and tilted the room. Colored it,
too, with its own bright darkness. The Concerto's first movement ended in a ripple of metal raindrops, tin thunder shaken
from the harpsichord.

The abrupt silence, a kind of reverse thunderclap, was
pierced by a hissing voice: "1769, you fool."

Skipwith recognized the voice and, as the second movement
started, muttered to himself—or so he thought—"Good God."

"Not if He made them," she said, or must have said. Her
profile burned cool beside him in the shadows and she had not
turned her head.

"What?" he whispered.

43

"Not good." Again the words emanated from her without movement. It was too dim to see any expression (Newman liked it dim to emphasize he played without a score); so he listened to Bach's slow double pulse-beat under the tangle of melody. But Newman made those double notes sound like a cardiac crisis, and Skipwith's mind strayed over toward her. She had not been there when he groped, late, for a seat, leaving the bright dining room's last banter and brandy. She could not have sat with him on purpose, after their little half-conversation before dinner. He had first noticed her, but not her beauty, when she made a small stir in these sluggish waters.

He had been talking with the club's president, Thatcher Harris, who was rising to one of his better-prepared effects, a story whose climactic dialogue was broken for suspense by lightings, puffings, scrutinizings of cigar—along with the by-play of coughs and fumbles and cigars offered round—as the circle tightened in around him for the punch line. Skipwith saw through all the tricks of theater, but enjoyed them nonetheless. He had seen Harris winch students around him that way, converting them to his own one noble passion, the works of Joseph Addison. This Cato gave his "little senate" laughs, not laws.

But that night he barely got to his second flick of a lighter when the bibulous scholars sensed rather than saw a flash of blue in and through them. Harris gaped with a vacant face as his cigar blurred over to the window; she had to fumble with the casement before she threw it out.

"Dr. Johnson, thou shouldst be living at this hour," Harris prayed with mock fervor. (Actually, everyone knew he was the one who changed the all-male rules of the Buttonites so she could enter.)

"*He* would be the freak, the dog on hind legs, in our world," she said with something approaching anger. Some thought her the best student Harris ever had, but she was the one least bullied by his jollity. As she turned toward the bar with hostile energy, her dress played around her with blue lightings.

Skipwith laughed through the mutilated end of Harris's story, and went over to the woman. It was easy to find her, vivid in the masculine hum and dimness. And that disturbed him. He loved the group for its dimness.

"Excuse me. My name is Gregory Skipwith, and I want to thank you for rescuing us from Thatch's cigar. Women can get away with what we men want to do; but we lack the nerve."

"I guess that's our use at these eighteenth-century gatherings. Though why I say 'ours' I can't imagine. There's only one of 'us.'"

"Well, thank God for the one. You are blessedly out of place."

"Why more than you? Or don't you think women read?"

It was then he noticed her beauty; how, against her blue dress, the green eyes startled. They seemed forced apart, or subtly crossed, by sheer force of concentration. Though they moved together in the literal sense, they somehow declared their independence—of each other, and of everything.

"Oh, I know you read." He knew, in fact, she had published a study of Lady Mary Wortley Montagu's politics.

"How do you know?" Was she fishing for a compliment? If so, he would make her work for it.

"Well, for one thing, you're here."

"Perhaps by false pretense. I may be a spy."

"A spy at Button's would soon die of boredom. In fact, I'm sure you know more about Addison than I do. Everyone here does."

"Not if you were Harris's pupil."

"Not pupil, admirer."

"Oh? I heard you were here because of him."

"Well, because of him at one remove. Because of Scott." The

late Noel Scott had been Harris's teacher, and the best friend of Skipwith's father.

"Then you never saw our great man snakecharm a classroom."

"I have seen him make any room he enters a classroom, including Scott's library. He kept trying to teach his own teacher."

"I hope Scott didn't let him."

"Oh yes. He loved it."

"They all do," she said with a mixed smile.

"You must, too. You're here because he broke the rules for you."

"Oh, he's a good rule-breaker, all right!" And the laugh this time was not bitter. She took his arm, to go back to the bar. "Do you teach, like everyone else here?"

"Quite the opposite. I unteach."

"How's that?"

"I tried to write novels, but—to Scott's great sorrow—ended up writing jingles, press releases, and corporate thank-you letters. But—who knows—maybe Addison was the real father of advertising."

"I suppose it pays a great deal."

"A subversive great deal. A dime a word for art; a dollar for seduction. And what of you—are you seducible?"

"Not by words, even of the dollar brand."

"I knew you were out of place here."

"Not good enough with words?"

"No, we covered that. You just seem more Scriblerian than Buttonite. A jolly hater like Pope or Swift, not a cold admirer. This place seemed almost too feminine for you. Your entry made it masculine."

"Eve in your little boys' Eden?"

"If so, oh happy fall. Even to the Scriblerians' level."

"Scriblerians for interest, Buttonites for courtesy, you

mean? Like 'Hell for friends and Heaven for the dogma'?"

"Yes. Pope, the little monster, was more interesting. But dull and yielding Addison was right."

"I'm not a yielder, then?"

"Apparently not. That's why I say you don't belong here. We tell our truths very dully."

"You also flirt clumsily."

"It's a field where expertise is suspect."

"Where everything is suspect." She walked off with that sudden way of hers. And that made him wonder why, in the half-empty library, he found her at his side two hours later.

Newman finished the slow movement—by now the pulse beat had become two bullets shot, again and again, through the fabric of the melody. Skipwith looked around to see if the whisperer would strike again. He didn't, but, just as Skipwith thought, the man was not paying attention to the music. He was trying to read an envelope in the dark, and as Skipwith watched, the man beside him wrote a word or two on it. They might have been playing tic-tac-toe to the Italian Concerto's rhythms.

The woman had not turned her head, but he ventured: "Our quarreling scholars."

"Our squirrelly ringers, you mean."

"Yes, they do seem out of place here."

"Like me?" she smiled, with malice, and finally turned her head.

The third movement was kicked off in a shower of sparks. Newman seemed to light the dark room with his own and the music's energy. Skipwith thought it appropriate the two behind him should defy Bach's power, drawn together in the endless feud that bored everyone but themselves.

They were the first he heard when he entered that night, just as in previous years. They were at the nuts and cheese table, expostulating through the crackers, in a shower of footnotes and cheddar. They made up a dwarf kingdom of their own, the tweedledeedumdom of Boswell-Johnson studies. Their scholarly rudeness was famous in print, and they kept up the battle wherever they met—even at this tame annual meeting of Addison lovers. Skipwith never understood how they met the entrance requirements. Eighteenth-century scholarship was not the issue. If it were, Skipwith would not belong. One had to be an Addisonian in Harris's enthusiastic way, cultivating a civilized diffidence. Weasel One and Weasel Two (that was how Skipwith thought of them) were rarely civilized and never diffident. Harris was bound to be uncomfortable around people who talked even more than he did, and only to each other, and angrily. They must have been the only members not recruited, one way or another, by Harris.

Weasel One, all eyebrows and a hunch of shoulder, believed that Boswell had slyly diminished Johnson while stealing from him. Weasel Two, even shorter than One but bulkier, felt Boswell had, in effect, invented Johnson, had made a neurotic pedant live beyond his merits in a blaze of artistry. Like evil Cheerybles they fed each other's obsessions, turning out oddments of knowledge useful to others while they waged their essentially useless war.

Newman finished, twirled his stool to face applause, tucked his stockinged feet beneath him, bowed his head, and pointed prayer-hands between his eyes as if to shoot himself with a finger-bullet. His closed eyes prolonged the ragged clapping, and Skipwith turned to her. "Tonight is our masculine night."

"You didn't like it?"

"He seems to think 'Italian' can mean nothing but Corsican."

"Why not be masculine?"

"Unrelievedly? The first movement has a masculine prance followed by a feminine tune, with delicate leaf turns. He twirled it like a top."

"That's why I liked it. Beauty always has to be rescued from sentimentality."

"Like yours?"

That stopped her for a second. "Not bad," she admitted. "You're flirting better"—and went off.

Skipwith had to find a bathroom—they had all been filled just after dinner. This private mansion-turned-scholars'-library rarely had so many people in it. Each year the host member had to find a congenial setting in his city, and this year was Walters's turn. They had come to Cambridge, since Walters taught at Harvard; and he had found this little-known old home.

In the small bathroom with one stool, Skipwith stood behind Weasel One, who was mumbling away as if Weasel Two were down in the bowl and had to be instructed as well as irrigated. When he turned around, Skipwith, to make conversation, said politely, "What is 1769?"

Weasel One looked as if he had been attacked; as if only Weasel Two's rudeness was part of his established order. He took kindness like a blow.

"Oh, just a crackbrained idea of Brown's—that Boswell published an anonymous Scottish pamphlet that year, and Junius stole its best lines."

"That's pretty horrendous, all right," Skipwith teetered between sympathy and teasing—but the Weasel looked genuinely relieved to find an ally. "I'm so glad you think so," he said to the washbowl.

Back in the library, with the lights on, Skipwith looked for Walters, to thank him for the evening's arrangements. But Walters was trying to do the Harris cigar routine—a dreary sight. The clumsiness only worked if it was feigned, not real. He waved at Walters through the smoke, and went to get his coat.

But there was Harris, with another circle, and Skipwith could not resist one last bit of the eighteenth-century chitchat he treasured (without getting all the references).

"Ah, Gregory." Harris opened a way for him with a gesture.

"How did you like friend Anthony's performance?"

"Very much," he lied. Newman was in the circle. "But Morton and Brown could not stop arguing, even for Bach."

"What was it this time?"

"I don't know. I asked Morton in the john just now, but he put me off with some Boswell story."

"Have you read this evening's memorial?" Every year the club published a special monograph for each member. This year's was on Addison's coffee house, Button's.

"I haven't read it yet, but it has a handsome cover."

"Llad here did it." Nathaniel Llad was the only Harris student who taught at Harris's university, Wisconsin. Blond and outdoorsy in this oldish group, he turned at mention of his name, and asked Skipwith quietly, "What was that Morton told you about 1769?"

"Oh, just the Boswell business again." If anyone knew what was going on in the Weasel's field, it was Llad. "Think there is anything to the Junius reference?"

"Not a thing," Llad said emphatically. He was less fanatical than the Weasels, but had the same lack of humor.

At the coat closet, Skipwith found himself beside the woman. "I know your last name, but not your first," he said.

"It's Lynn, short for Cymbeline."

"A Shakespearean father?"

"No, mother. You still think women cannot read?"

"Of course not. But I guess that is what my question meant."

"No, it meant: 'Will you talk to me?' "

"Fair enough. Will you?" Perhaps they could have a drink together at the hotel.

"What about?"

"For Christ's sake, about anything. Don't you get tired of verbal fencing?"

She gave him a blank look. Answered: "Yes." And went out the door.

Skipwith turned down Toller's offer of a ride, put on his coat, decided to walk off the brandy and the stuffy rooms. He headed for Harvard Yard. The students' windows were closed against a cold spring night, though rock music buzzed through them, made the place hum like a honeycomb. He was wistful for his own school days, and feeling a little self-pity. The night had not been quite the respite he looked forward to at Button's. Even Harris's recycled jokes were normally restful, and they had bored him tonight. Was it the woman's presence? He feared he would have to settle in for some real despondency this year. Then he remembered: this was his first night at Button's since his wife Mary had left him. He had met her here, during his one year at Harvard (before being drafted for Korea). Better get back to the hotel after all. He went out of the yard for a cab.

The kiosks and subway entry had a kind of trashy elegance by night, erotic little hearths to beat off the chill of learning. He felt a subtle twitch of his loins toward the lurid magazines, vivid at a distance, squalid up close. The browsers were lit yellow from below as by Lautrec footlights. He strolled past a cab and into the milky white glare of an all-night coffee shop; ordered a large black coffee to go, and came out fighting the little plastic top off the flimsy cardboard. The coffee was spiced and redolent mud. He looked for a place to dump it; stepped into an alley. The hiss of the coffee on the wall made him conscious of a lumbar pressure. "God, I'm suggestible," he thought and zipped down his fly.

He had just begun to relieve himself when the wall flew out at him. His brain was working with odd clarity but in slow motion as he tasted the blood from his nose. The wall was still there. Something had thrown him at it. The ache in his back and his nose had come simultaneously. He could see nothing; but hands, three hundred it seemed, were rummaging in his clothes. Finally, blinking like a mole, he made out a shape and grabbed for it. It kicked him in the ribs. He tried to shout and couldn't; he would have to work at the job of pulling a breath. When it did come, it hurt as much as the paralyzed breathlessness had.

"Keep it up," he heard. So there were two of them. He felt the other's fumbling, but still saw only one shape, the one that had kicked him and spoken. It was entirely black. Then he felt the nuzzling of a sock near his neck. He reached for it, as if to distract himself from the pain, and it melted in his hands.

"Look out!" the kicker said; and Skipwith heard a whine from his melting intimate. At last he did get out a weak "Help!"; there was noise at the alley's mouth; and the kicker turned away. The melter turned too, but Skipwith now had a new handful of stocking cloth, the stuff he seemed made of, and held on, roughly dragged toward the light. The man turned to hit at his grasp, and the two caught each other's eyes with a mutual petrifaction. It was Weasel One.

ii

Skipwith was licking at his blood abstractedly, a stocking cap in his hand, when the students picked him up. They tried to call an ambulance, but he asked to go to his hotel. One boy went with him in the cab, and had to argue the bloody sight past a doorman. The student got him into bed and wiped the blood off his face. Skipwith woke later that night, vomiting blood, tried to reach the phone, and fainted. Later he got to the phone by setting his whole side on fire with the reach, said "Help," and fainted again.

When he woke in the hospital, the student was there, asking if there was someone he could call. "What's the matter with me?" The doctor had told the student: a broken rib, a herniated diaphragm, a broken nose, and one lost tooth. Skipwith felt back toward the fire, which was returning. His whole upper body was wrapped tight.

The doctor came in, and the boy left. "We called your company; they asked if they could send you anything." No. He toyed with the idea of giving his ex-wife's new name and address, but could not muster that degree of self-pity. There was, as well, no need to bother Caroline, at the apartment. They specialized in not bothering each other. He drifted off to sleep again, till he heard a voice.

"You were right about one thing."

"What?" he asked, trying to open his eyes.

"It was a bit too masculine an evening."

"Cymbeline?"

"Lynn."

"Fair enough, if you call me Gregory, not Greg."

"Done."

"Done."

He couldn't think of anything else to say, and she just sat there, as if she had long ago made herself at home.

"How did you know?"

"I heard."

"Before people left on Saturday? Does Harris know?"

"I don't think so. What happened?"

"I don't know."

"The police who brought you here said you kept mumbling something about weasels."

"I must have been swearing at the rats who did this." He was tempted to tell her about Weasel One, but she probably wouldn't believe him. Besides, he already felt an instinct to save the Weasel and everything about him. He was his.

"Tell me about it." She looked different, less a thing of edges than last night. He was tempted.

"There's nothing to tell. I got mugged." He shrugged, and then winced.

"I thought you didn't like the tough guy pose."

"I thought you did."

"Don't you get tired of this verbal fencing?"

He tried to laugh, disastrously. He could taste some blood when he coughed, but didn't tell her. Oddly, he did like the tough guy pose for a change. But he dissembled on an instinct: "God, do I ever hate it. That's why I like the delicate and retiring Addison."

"Yes, a nice little old lady of a man. He almost made Whiggism make sense."

"Is that the best you can say of him?"

She looked truly startled at his obtuseness. "That is the worst I can say of him."

His head was crumbling in some chambers he did not know he had, and he slept.

When he woke, mumbling, she had leaned over him, alert and looking as she had last night.

"Trying to hear my secrets?" He said it jokingly, and was shocked to see her subtly crossed eyes straighten themselves with an effort much like hate. He wanted her out. He called the nurse for a sleeping pill to keep him from talking.

The next morning he checked out, against the doctor's orders, and went back to his hotel. He tried to pack his bag, but felt the chambers going dead again in his brain. He splashed water on his face, and went down to the bar for a drink. It was one of those hotels with a great empty core up the middle. He sat islanded by an ornamental pool near the central bar, and heard conversations cross and mingle above him, too dim to be made out. A parrot, hung in a cage, made ugly sounds.

"Give me a Scotch."

"It's ten o'clock, sir, the bar does not open till eleven."

"Get me a drink! Can't you see I'm dying? This is on doctor's orders!" He was mad, and it cleared the brain. That was a feeling he could learn to like. The waiter went for his Scotch. The meeting at Button's had not been so bad after all. He would have no time, just yet, for despondency.

He wondered if the Weasel was having trouble keeping his mind on the course he taught at Columbia. The adrenalin was doing as much to restore him as the Scotch. It normally paralyzed him with embarrassment to argue with a rude cabbie. But anger braced him now. Getting Weasel would give his life purpose.

But what of the girl? Why had the Weasel told her? (It had to be that. He had asked the student if anything was in the paper, and no one had inquired for him at the hotel desk *but* the student). He knew of no tie between Lynn (he thought of her already by her first name) and the weaselly Morton. Harris would know. Perhaps he should call Wisconsin. But first he had to get back to New York. This time he packed the whole bag before collapsing on the bed. When he woke, a few hours later, he headed for Logan Airport, going home.

iii

"Home." New York had never been that to him, even before Mary left. They lived in Pelham, and he commuted to work. His time in the apartment since then could not be called living, despite Caroline. Anger at rattling around Manhattan behind mad cabbies suddenly boiled over and he said: "I have taped-up ribs, and if you take another corner like that I'll vomit blood all over this cab." To his amazement, the driver slowed down and apologized.

He realized, at that moment, why New York is such a murderous city. Not for its homicide rate—less, in proportion, than that of Houston or whatnot. The air is thick with murders uncommitted, violences not done for lack of time or focus. Most of its murders are still trying to happen.

At the apartment house he left his bag for the doorman. The slow little elevator scraped up one side with its customary shearing sound. He came into the hall's odorous aftermath of last night's dinners and realized how tired he was of stepping over and through the residue of other people's lives.

Caroline met him at the door and tried to hug him. The pain was so intense he pushed her, hard—he might as well have hit her. He apologized, did not mean it. He had told the hotel not to take her calls. He didn't know why. He felt some real break had to be made from his life, from this apartment, from the endless cabs and smelly elevators. He told her he had been mugged, and might be going to Wisconsin. They both came and went with minimal signals, but it had been comfortable to have her there. Too comfortable. He got a Scotch and crawled into bed. When she sat on the mattress, his side flared—as it did whenever he shifted. He got out and lay flat on the floor. It made him feel somehow pure, despite the wooziness. He felt reborn with anger. Harris might calm him down again. Maybe he could explain it all. Why did he feel a sudden disappointment at that thought? Should he see Weasel One before he called Harris? Where was the girl, he wondered. Back at her Virginia estate? Maybe he'd straighten her eyes for good, or learn to return their hate.

Next morning he called the Weasel at Columbia. But the secretary of the English Department said he had taken a sudden leave, to visit a sick parent. The secretary could not tell him where the parent lived, but Skipwith knew Weasel Two taught at Chapel Hill. When he reached him there, Weasel Two was suspiciously affable, had heard nothing of Skipwith's being mugged, and knew nothing of Weasel One's whereabouts. It looked like he would have to call Harris, after all. No, better go see him. Spend a day to catch up at the office, and take one of the week's vacations coming to him. (He had taken none since his wife first asked for the divorce.)

That night, Caroline was at the ballet. Skipwith, as usual, was watching TV. His resolve to leave the apartment had begun to wane as he lived in its dulling influence. Why look for trouble? Whatever the Weasel was up to, he had made some mistake. He searched for something Skipwith didn't have. Nothing was missing from his pockets when the hospital returned his clothes. The event seemed unreal already; only the pain in his side brought it back to him, in the morning, vividly. It made him want to wake up. But now he was dozing when the phone rang.

"Gregory? Thatch Harris here. How are you?"

"I'm all right. How did you learn?"

"Learn what?"

"Oh, nothing. I thought you might have heard I was mugged after our At Button's meeting."

"*No*, my dear boy. Nothing bad, is it?"

"No, I'm recovered."

"I'm calling about a little skulduggery being planned by your firm."

"By Continent?"

"It's your student marketing line. I've asked permission to address the board. Didn't ask you to intercede because I don't want to involve you in any acrimony I might cause."

"Don't worry about that. Are you coming here for the board meeting?"

"Yes." Gregory did not remember when the board met, but knew it was soon. He offered Harris a bed in the apartment, and was glad when he turned it down. Caroline would be awkward. He was used to meeting Harris only in male gatherings, and felt somehow like a schoolboy in his company. "What's the matter with the student products?"

"Your Mr. Wingate is a bit of a rascal, I fear."

"Of course he is. But he's damn good at his rascality."

"Well, perhaps we can outrascal him for a better cause. A bit more Kit-Cat work than Button's, don't you think?"

(God! Skipwith laughed. He even plots in literary terms.)

Wingate had come to Continent under something of a cloud.

He had been involved in record company payola schemes—
not, apparently, bribing disc jockeys himself, but tapping the
phones of rivals who did. Skipwith wondered what racy work
he could dig up in a staid company like Continent Books.

iv

Monday, after his week of convalescence, Skipwith went to
the sales meeting. Coffee steam fought different brands of
cologne. It brought back a hundred morning meetings of
backslapping bluster, comparison of golf scores, the gleam of
the coffee urn and of manicured fingernails. He wondered if
one can die of an Old Spice overdose. No one asked his golf
score. No one had asked him anything for over a year—his
weekends were a lineup of TV shows.

Skipwith was silent as usual. And Wingate, as usual, was
surly. He always looked overhung, and often was; but you
could not count on it. He made some of his surest moves when
he looked as if he had come there straight from the gutter.
Everyone at Continent hated him. Except, perhaps, everyone's boss, George Wolfson—who feared him.

Skipwith didn't dislike Wingate. He only hated him ex of-
ficio. They were, in effect, the company's freakish opposites.
Skipwith, on the basis of one good review of his unread Korean
war novel, had been hired to placate the Old Man, George
Wolfson's father; to service old accounts; to keep the advertising dignified. Continent Books had been founded as a hobby by
the Old Man, who used the book importing business as an
excuse to tour Europe every year. But his son, George, had
made it a supplier of cards and games to stationery stores, and
begun the expansion that brought Wingate to the firm. Wingate knew the campus bookstores from his rock record days.
And he would never get another job in the music business.

By the time George Wolfson shepherded the eight men to

their chairs around the table, each bringing his last cup of coffee, Wingate had taken his customary seat by the wall. He rarely said anything here, and liked to underline his outsider role.

Carlson had tried out some new game idea over the weekend. "This one is called Dostoievski. My own kids couldn't pronounce it, but they liked playing murders and secret agents. There was more Ellery Queen than Raskolnikov in the way the plots worked; but the name gives it an exotic literary touch."

Wolfson suggested they give it a trial run; no one argued; that was how the table "voted." Stephen Luck said the run should be only five thousand or so, since this was really the same, except for names and visuals, as the CIA game they had put out last year. "That's its advantage," Wolfson said. "People want the same thing over and over, just dressed up in different ways." (Wingate was always telling him that.) "In fact, why not put out an Ellery Queen game in six months. Six months after that, a Nero Wolfe, and so on. The secret is to find the right formula, then vary it." (Wolfson learned well.)

Skipwith had heard enough; he would have to put a literary veneer on some of the ads, the only ads shown the Old Man. He said he had to make a call, and went for his office. Only at the door of it did he notice Wingate was following him. He waved him past his secretary. Wingate didn't take the chair offered him, but paced—lounged, rather—around the office.

"Getting so you can't take the gentlemen bullshitters on an empty stomach?"

"Is that what you think of them?"

"I think if Wolfson smelt something funny and asked any one of them, 'Did you fart?' he'd get the answer, 'No, chief, do you want me to?' "

"For God's sake, why don't you say that some morning? It would make my day."

"What's got into you?"

"What do you mean?"

"You seem to have acquired balls somewhere."

For a moment Skipwith bridled—so he didn't have them before? "Balls! I didn't get balls. I just got beat up."

"That'll do it. I always thought you gave the bullshitters their gentlemanly cover. Something in your eyes back there made me think you might be getting tired of the funny card racks in stationery stores." Skipwith remembered Dave Frank's effort to give Wingate the Rorschach test required of all executives at Continent. (Frank was the psychologist who invented subliminal messages for greeting cards.) Poor Frank was fuming for a week because Wingate gave the same answer to every one of the inkblots: "They're your balls, all right, Frank. I wonder who cut them off?"

"What's on your mind, Ben?" He only noticed as he said it that this was the first time he had called him anything but Wingate.

"I'm playing a hunch. I've got George half sold on a new idea, and he's bound to try it out on you as its enemy presumptive. My hunch is that you have more reason to resent all this literary posing and gentlemanly crap than anyone. You know better than most how fake it is."

"You mean I'm the literary whore?"

"Take it as flattery. The sincerest flattery is always built on insult. That's why Frank puts out all those insult cards for birthdays. You know, where calling your mother a weirdo proves you trust her to be understanding and that she trusts you to love even a weirdo."

"Yeah, only I happen to know you gave Frank that idea because you thought he was dumb enough to buy it."

"So did thousands of other people."

"I didn't. I don't."

"Okay, be difficult. When can I see Harris?"

"How did you know he was coming?"

"I know."

"He's supposed to meet with the board tomorrow."

"I want to see him first."

"Why don't you ask him?"

"I thought he might pay more attention to a fellow Button-ite."

"You do know things." He had never mentioned At Button's around the office, and never seen Wingate elsewhere.

"I'm having lunch with him. If he wants to see you, I'll call you to join us."

"Fair enough. Tell me something about him."

"You mean you don't know?"

Wingate grinned: "Maybe I'm just checking."

"On him, or on me?"

"On the odd coupling."

"Flattery by insult? Well, Harris is the most successful teacher I ever met. I know that, though I was never in his classroom. His students are everywhere, and identify themselves as that. Only his special favorites join At Button's. I was a friend of a favorite who refused to join."

"Why?" It was Wingate's first sign of unguarded interest.

"Thought it was too barmy, as he put it, a lot of grown men making believe they are back in the eighteenth century."

"I like your friend."

"Hmmmm, I don't think Scott would have liked you."

"Insult without flattery?"

"I was talking about Scott. I don't know what I think of you."

"Just call me a weirdo and I'll know you love me. Go on with Harris."

"In his sixties. Wife long dead. Never published anything, not even on Addison."

"Didn't that stand in his way at Wisconsin?"

"He went there with an established reputation. Scott told

me there was some trouble before then, I don't know why." He thought a moment. Then it occurred to him: "Do you?"

Wingate just smiled. Why was Skipwith assuming that Wingate knew everything he was telling him? No wonder others in the office thought Wingate was up to his old tricks of tapping phones.

"I'll be in my office if you call." Wingate left, and Skipwith began the series of phone calls he must finish by one o'clock.

v

Harris was waiting for him at the restaurant—a typical business lunch place with crisp white linen and French bread—where it was a point of gamesmanship to buy an expensive bottle of wine and leave it half finished. Harris stood out by his pallor—the other men were trim but ruddy, with a thin overlay of tan they got from sunlamps. Harris was so tweedy and professorial—to the very tufts in his ears and the shag of his floppy hat—that it gave people a start when he reached for his cigar rather than a pipe.

After the amenities, Skipwith relayed Wingate's request.

"I'd rather not see him. I don't want there to be anything personal in my opposition to him at your company's meeting."

"What's he up to?"

"I don't have all the details. But a number of the better book dealers on campuses have banded together to fight the takeover of stores by these new chains. They replace books with more expensive gadgetry like calculators and cassettes. Wingate has come up with a plan to do the distributing for a dozen or so manufacturers, and to underwrite the development of video tape twaddle to soak up all that student money out there."

"I didn't notice any money around when I went to school."

"My boy, you would shudder to see what students bring to

school now. They arrive as freshmen with their own calculators, and then trade up for more expensive ones. Movie equipment alone is becoming a million-dollar business on campuses. There are schools now where you cannot buy a single book except assigned texts and the college outline series. The very citadel of civilization is peddling barbarism on a supermarket basis."

Harris, waxing eloquent, always provided imaginative touches; but Skipwith could see how this would touch Harris where he lived.

"How do you expect to counter Wingate's pitch? It sounds like the breakthrough young Wolfson has been looking for."

"Yes, but Wolfson senior is going to be at the board meeting; and I know he is on the side of the angels. In fact, I never told you this, but I recommended you to Frederick Wolfson. He told George to hire you."

"Well, thanks, but I wish I could have thanked you sooner. Why didn't you tell me?"

"One hates to boast of every littlest favor done."

"Yes, but one likes to know one's footing, and . . . Well, thanks anyway." He was doing it again. Making him feel like a schoolboy in need of better grades. "I'll go tell Wingate not to come."

"Tell him I wouldn't mind seeing him after the meeting."

On the phone, Wingate said with a growl, "Oh, he *will*, will he?" when Skipwith said Harris would see him after talking to the board. Back at the table, Skipwith got to the line of questioning he had rehearsed off and on while making his phone calls that morning.

"Do you remember our last At Button's, toward the end of the evening, when I came over to say goodbye?"

"Vaguely," he frowned. "I always go a bit heavy on the brandy at my favorite affair."

"Who was in that group besides you and Llad?"

"I know I can't remember that. Why?"

"I said something about Thomas Morton that may have led to my getting mugged that night."

"My dear boy, that's impossible. You *were* hit on the head, weren't you?"

"Very well and proper," he grinned sourly. "I get my new tooth tomorrow. But that is what puzzled me. I can't imagine Thomas Morton doing anything efficiently; yet he was one of those who mugged me. He didn't have time to go get help. The only person who saw me turn around during Morton's outburst was Lynn Baker. I can imagine her doing almost anything efficiently, but not beating me up. It must have been one of those I mentioned Morton to in that last circle around you."

"I can ask Llad if he remembers. He is in town on some business of his own, so we are sharing a hotel room. But I'm sure you must be mistaken. It was dark, you had a bloody nose, your eyes must have been swollen . . ."

"One eye was, but . . ."

"There are a thousand tricks the mind can play in bad light and panicky moments. Your thoughts probably flashed back to Morton's face as you had seen it earlier that evening. Did you see him in the dark?"

"Yes, while Newman was playing."

"You see? A very natural flicker of association. Your mind, lacking any image to go with the unexpected, just slipped back to an earlier slide, as it were. We have to explain things to ourselves, even the inexplicable, you know."

"But the Weasel explained nothing. That was the shock, not a cure for shock."

"The what?"

"Oh, the Weasel, that's how I've always thought of Morton."

"Yes," he laughed. "One can see why. But that just makes it more likely that you would associate him with an unpleasant thing happening right after you met him again—an alley rat is not so far from a weasel, after all."

"Well, maybe. But . . ." He was unconvinced; but it is hard to argue while feeling like a schoolboy. Besides, there was something in what Harris said. He would think about it.

"And now that we have solved that little puzzle, how about rewarding ourselves with a really *good* brandy?"

vi

Back in the office, he reviewed his doubts about the Harris explanation, and found them dissolving, one by one, in the brandy fumes. What did he have to go on after all? The glimpse in a dark scuffle would not have stood up against a good lawyer's skeptical questioning. That is one reason he had been reserving the Weasel for himself—he knew the law would not be any use here. But he had not recognized that there was a good reason for the law's uselessness—the lack of real evidence. He had been a damn fool. He thought how happy he was that Caroline would be in the apartment tonight, not Harris.

His secretary buzzed: "Mr. Wingate to see you."

"I've been checking some things since I talked to you. Call Harris."

"Why?"

"He'll want to see me now."

"Then call him yourself."

"He'll want to see you, too."

"I've got an appointment tonight."

"This won't take long."

Skipwith had his secretary call Harris's room. Llad answered. "He'll do," said Wingate, and took the phone from Skipwith's hand. "We never met, mister ski-instructor. But if Harris doesn't see me tonight, Skipwith here is going to learn why he got beat up." He hung up.

"You're not waiting for an answer?"

"Only Harris can give it. He'll give it soon."

"What's this about my mugging?"

"What did Harris tell you?"

"He made sense of it at last." He felt surer of that now than when he had tried to make himself believe it.

"What'd he say?"

"He said I was bound to make a mistake about who beat me up—in that light, with a bad eye and a bleeding nose."

"Did you have a bloody nose?"

"Yes."

"Did you tell him that?"

A pause. "No."

"Who did?"

"I suppose he was supposing."

"I suppose," Wingate said with a sigh. The phone rang.

"Gregory, this is Thatch. Your friend must be even crazier than I had heard. But since he brings you into it, I would be glad to see him for drinks here at the hotel around five."

"What about me?"

"I think it would be best for you to skip this one, old boy."

"I'm coming," he snapped, and hung up. *"Goddamit, why does everyone around here know more about my life than I do?"* He was surprised at the resonance that filled out his voice. His secretary came running in to see if he and Wingate were fighting.

"What's this all about, Wingate?"

"You got me. I was just playing a hunch. I checked with some old contacts of mine, who said Morton and Harris go way back. Then I found that Morton disappeared on the night you were mugged and can't be found by his university. Other teachers in his department are mad as hell at having to take over his courses. I thought there might be a connection. It was worth a try."

"And that's all you have to tell me?"

"Play your cards right, and it'll pry the rest out of Harris. Or enough for you to find out elsewhere. His phone call tells you I was onto something. I don't care about that, though. I just want to make an honest buck."

"For a change?"

Wingate shrugged.

At the hotel, Harris invited them up to his room. Llad was at the sideboard, with a plentiful bar. "We're having some of the board members over for lunch after tomorrow's meeting."

"You don't have to apologize for booze to me."

"I'm sure I don't, Mr. Wingate. What's all this about Mr. Skipwith's accident?"

"That's between you and him. All I'm interested in is teaching aids."

"That's what you call those toys?"

"Beats readin', doesn't it?"

"How would you know?"

Wingate turned to Skipwith. "This guy's another flatterer."

"Frankly, Mr. Wingate, I consider you a threat to civilization, what little is left of it. I cannot beat the idiot box by taking on TV networks. But I think I can beat a disreputable character like you. I mean to tell the board tomorrow some things even *it* did not know about your work for the record industry."

Wingate moved forward but Llad stepped in and challenged him: "Keep it up!"

But Wingate was smiling. "Then the kid here will learn about his schoolmaster's alley work."

Skipwith's neck hairs had pricked at the words "Keep it up." He couldn't believe it, but couldn't doubt it, either. As soon as his head had partly cleared, he threw himself forward. "It was *you*, you bastard!" The last word was choked off by Llad's flat hand that cut across the side of his neck and made him think his windpipe had been severed. Llad was following Skipwith as he staggered back, when Wingate caught his belt from behind.

Llad spun with his hand scything but checked it just as it touched the knifeblade Wingate had produced from his pocket. "Cool off, ski-instructor," Wingate said. Holding Llad's belt with one hand, he calmly sawed through it with the other, just nicking his skin all the while to keep him still, then lowered his pants just enough to hobble him, and went for the door.

"Wait," Skipwith tried to say, but no words came; he was still fighting to breathe. Wingate grabbed his wrist and Skipwith suddenly realized how strong this bleary-eyed five-and-a-half-footer was. Wingate dragged him out the door.

A block away, in a bar, Skipwith could breathe again at last. His hands were shaking violently as he lifted the glass with both of them. "What's it all about?"

"You got me." Wingate was genuinely puzzled. "It must be bigger than anything I guessed. *Much* bigger, and I wouldn't have brought it up. What's a million dollars here or there? I can find a different gimmick." He shrugged. "No more teaching aids. By the way, what do you think of that blond teacher's aid?"

"Let's go back."

"Without me, pal. That guy knows what he's doing."

"It was a lucky punch. He just missed my jaw."

"He chose his spot. Why break a hand on your thick skull? If you ever mix with him again, be sure not to fight fair. He's a pro."

"He's *the* pro—the one in the alley."

"Yeah? Then I can see why you would want to get back at him. But if I were you, I would avoid him for a while, and see what Harris is willing to tell you. Me, I gotta go think up a different way to make a million." Skipwith tried to thank him as Wingate got up to leave, but he was having trouble with his windpipe again.

Back at the apartment, Harris called. "Let me explain, dear fellow. Tomorrow for dinner, the same restaurant we had lunch at?"

"Will Llad be there?"

"No."

"Then I will. I don't know why. You Addisonians play too rough for me." Harris laughed uncertainly, hoping he meant it as a joke. He didn't.

vii

The same crisp bread and linen, but lower lights—and the wine bottles were being finished now. He noticed that Harris had taken an isolated table this time, off on the side. "You'll be happy to hear that my meeting with your board went quite satisfactorily."

"Yeah, I heard. We lost several million dollars by your visit."

"But think what civilization gained."

"I wonder, after your learned goon civilized my windpipe."

"A regrettable accident, but one entirely explicable."

"You talked to me of inexplicables last time. Are you going to deny that Llad was in that alley, too?"

"No, alas, he was there. A headstrong young man, despite his knowledge of Augustan club life."

"He belongs in the Hellfire Club, not Button's."

"Exactly, and for some of the same reasons that government spies hung around that den of thieves and geniuses."

"You're going to tell me Llad's a spy?"

"Well, an agent."

Skipwith laughed enough to attract notice.

"What's the joke?"

"She told me *she* was a spy, and I thought it an absurd thing at Button's."

"She? Lynn? Actually, she is an agent, too."

Skipwith laughed again, not as heartily. "Are they all spooks then? Was I the only idiot believing it was what it pretended to be?"

"No, there are only five agents in the club—quite by accident, by the way. I would have preferred to keep them out."

"I should hope so. Let me see, Llad and Lynn and Morton—and you?"

"Oh, me, of course, dear boy."

"Who's the other? Walters?"

"No, as a matter of fact, it's Brown."

"You mean he and Morton are on the same side in something?"

"Oh, that was quite the most delightful part of the charade. They have always been on the same side, even about Boswell and Johnson."

"Two weasels of the same stripe, after all." Harris nodded. "Who you guys spying for?"

"The CIA, of course. Isn't everybody?"

"Everybody but me. Everybody knows things but me. Now that you spyers outnumber us spyees, can't you just call off the whole game?"

"Unfortunately not. There are some serious aspects even to so silly a thing as spying. It's hard to believe, I know—God, do I know! But there it is."

"What made me play my ignominious little part?"

"Llad always feared the club. He thought your weasel friends would give something away around people who really know their Johnson and Boswell. He was wrong, of course. Their scholarship is impeccable."

"Which one is the pretender?"

"They've never told—not even me. They rejoice in the perfection of their act. It made them especially convincing when they traveled to learned congresses, apart or as a team—well, as a traveling quarrel. Their passion for their subject seemed to preclude all other interests. Most spies are tripped up knowing too much. They knew too much about only one thing, and that lifted suspicion from them."

"I still don't understand how I came to give a tooth for the cause."

"You used an unfortunate phrase. The—er, weasels— delight in using their specialty as a code. If anyone finds the writings they carry, it is assumed they are connected with the ancient quarrel. One especially sensitive project they have in hand is called the Boswell Business. Llad thought you had picked that up as a technical term. He also told me later that you were talking about Julius, another of our agents. I informed him—too late, I'm sorry to say, to save your tooth—that it was Junius you were referring to. Then, when the envelope the 'weasels' were writing on was missing, you were the natural subject of suspicion. You saw them writing on it. They went after you to get the envelope back. If only they had consulted me first, I could have told them you were above subterfuge."

"Now there's some flattery I'm beginning to take as an insult."

"Eh?"

"Nothing, I'm just getting tired of being the innocent shuttlecock. So Lynn was sent to find out what I knew while I was still groggy?"

"Well," Harris laughed, "we could hardly send Morton, now, could we?"

"That makes me feel better about her."

"Why?"

"I liked her at the club, but not at the hospital." Harris raised his brows. "She was trying to be nice at the hospital, in order to be nosy. I liked her better mean."

"So do I. She is more trustworthy then."

"Are her growls at you an act, too?"

"No, I regret to say that she profoundly dislikes me. But we have our assignments."

"How did Wingate catch wind of you?"

"He's an ex—ex-CIA. Where do you think he acquired his admirable knowledge of electronics, so sadly prostituted on rock studios, phone taps, and—calculators," he shuddered.

"Then that's another animosity that's genuine."

"Yes, spies don't have to like each other, any more than priests do. As I reconstruct it, Wingate doesn't know much, actually. He worked once with Morton, and knew of my connection with the club. When he heard I was coming to see the board, he found out I had recommended you for your job, did a little check on you and your accident—it was enough to run a bluff."

"And it worked."

"He knew we were not bluffing when I said there was more to his rock music career than has come out. Some of that was for the Agency, so our hands are partly tied. But he does not know how much we might use if we have to."

"Lovely world you live in."

"It makes the world safe for you."

"And for Addison?"

"No, Addison would not survive very well now. That is why I love him so. He transports us to a different world entirely. Some people have detective novels for escape. I have Addison. You see, my boy, I still do believe in something. What I teach my students."

"Those you do not recruit as agents?"

"Even some of those I do. Llad, for instance. He is not only a scholar but a believer in the world he has explored. Did you read his monograph?"

"No. I don't think I will, now. How about Lynn?"

"Well, you said yourself she was not Addisonian—she told me of your conversation at the club. I'm afraid you're right."

Funny, Lynn was the one thing Skipwith began to think he could believe in.

"I don't suppose you can tell me what you are up to?"

"Oh no, dear fellow, all too hush-hush. The Agency is rather silly about that. Not really so derring-do as you might think. I know poor Llad regrets that the only time he has ever used his training in the rougher side of intelligence work—one I never mixed in—was on a hapless spectator. It is an occupational hazard. The only defense against official drivel is admitted rodomontade. Real spies have a shamefaced feeling, only part-confessed, that they are playing boys' games after all. They apologize for their pretensions, yet feel obliged to live up to them. The only real spy work is Tom Sawyer's death oath, the 'make-believe.' The reality is impregnated with doubt, and men can't be made to believe even in themselves."

"What's happened to Morton?"

"I'm afraid he's left us. He was rather upset at the sight of your blood—that's where I got a vivid report on your insulted nose. We spies lead sheltered lives, after all. He had been thinking of retiring, and this was the last straw. We took care of him."

Skipwith had trouble swallowing his wine. "You mean you *killed* him?"

Harris roared with laughter. "Of course not! We are not so dime-novel as that! We gave him a new identity. He had plenty of retirement pay coming. I expect we'll be reading some new Johnsonian articles by somebody we never heard of before."

"What will poor Brown do without him?"

"He may be looking for a new foe now. You wouldn't be interested?"

"No thanks." Skipwith was quiet for a while. "You know I was saving Morton up for me. There was one foe I could match."

"What a terrible thought to have after a night at Button's." He could tell that Harris was sincerely shocked. "By the way, I wouldn't mention any of this to anyone, not even Caroline."

"So you know about her."

"Yes, and I'm glad you've found someone after that distressing breakup with Mary."

"Yeah. Someone."

He wanted to tell Caroline, though. Tell someone. Maybe Wingate. Instead he went to a movie.

viii

Next day, at the office, Wingate poked his head in. "Harris straighten you out?"

"Yes."

"Give you a lot of CIA mumbo-jumbo?" He nodded. "D'ja believe it?" Another nod. "Why?"

"You should know." And here he broke his promise, slightly; told one thing *he* had been told. "After all, you're an ex-agent."

"Maybe I'm an ex-believer. Come to think of it, I'm ex— most things."

Skipwith began to feel closer to Wingate. They were almost partners-in-something. Not quite crime. And certainly not crime-busting. At any rate, they had lunch together fairly often. The office noticed and wondered. Finally, a secretary asked Wingate why they had become so chummy. "I think it's the way I handle a knife." She thought that was a funny answer, but she didn't laugh.

Others sounded out Skipwith, asking how he could side with Wingate. He answered: "He's a rainmaker. How can you hire such a man and not get thunder?"

As spring revived New York, Skipwith and Wingate often walked to the zoo and back at lunch hour, eating at a hot dog stand. "Got any new gimmick?" Skipwith asked once.

"What about exercise machines? Do you think college kids would buy exercise machines?"

"I think college kids are exercise machines."

Skipwith was quarreling with Caroline off and on, and Wingate noticed that he often brought up Lynn Baker. "Funny," he answered one day, "I remember reading something about her a long time ago."

"Probably about her father. He is some kind of Washington eminence."

"Probably."

For the rest they talked about books. Wingate was a secret reader. He asked that Skipwith not give him away at the office. "Not your stuffy eighteenth century, though. I prefer the rowdy English Renaissance—all the plots: the Babington Plot, Lopez Plot, Squier Plot, etc." To Skipwith's amazement, Wingate didn't like Shakespeare, but he read him constantly; trying to find evidence for the historical plots going on all around Burbage's hack writer. He read Shakespeare plays as if they were out-of-date newspapers written by not very bright reporters. "Anyone would have known more about the Bye Plot than Shakespeare revealed in *Measure for Measure*." The opposite extremes of Continent Books had met, but not in the center—somewhere off to the side. Skipwith was not fighting Wingate's more outrageous ideas now—perhaps because he was not coming up with many. They were not earning their keep by the time summer began. Skipwith remembered that he had not read Shakespeare in years, and when Caroline came home at night she normally found the TV off.

But it was not Wingate's bookishness that appealed to him. Without admitting it to himself, Skipwith *was* impressed by the way he handled a knife—that knife he had never seen again, though he knew (without asking) he still carried it. He tried to pump Wingate about his days as an agent. But all Wingate would do was make fun of the Agency—"one stupid fuck-up after another. If America were a business, we'd be bankrupt." Carlson the gamesman made the new office game guessing which was becoming more like the other, Skipwith like Wingate, or vice versa. Skipwith was even heard to say once, "This company's got no balls." But not in the hearing of either Wolfson.

At off daydreaming moments Skipwith was shamed with the thought that he missed having Weasel One to deal with. Not that he would, finally, have harmed him; he just missed thinking about what he *might* have done to him. But it was only a few weeks before excitement reentered his life. Harris called, and asked if Skipwith would represent At Button's in London for this year's Enlightenment Congress. Skipwith loved London, but had to catch up on some business. Harris said the other delegate would be Lynn Baker, and Skipwith suddenly found it a little hard to breathe. He'd go. "Does this have something to do with your other work?"

"You mean my teaching?" The tone was a rebuke, though the words were not. "Nothing at all, dear boy."

He hung up, looked around the office, found it somehow brighter than it was before, and went over to talk with Wingate.

By the time he got back to his office there was a message on his desk. A Miss Baker in Virginia had been trying to reach him. He called the number given, and a butler summoned Lynn. She didn't bother to answer his hello.

"You can't go."

"Can't what?"

"Can't go to London."

"Why?"

"You would get in my way."

"We don't have to travel together. We would not have to see each other except at the Congress—not even there, if you do not *want* to see me." He hoped he had not sounded as stuffy as he felt.

"Oh, don't be silly. It's too complicated to discuss on the phone. Where can I meet you, there or here?"

"There," he answered. He had always wanted to see how rich people live.

ix

He landed in Washington with a quickening pulse. Fuzzy spring had clicked into focus and found itself articulated summer. Washington's bogus Greek and Roman temples shrank partly back to scale under a blue sky large as the Mediterranean's. Lynn had told him the drive to her Virginia estate was too complicated for a stranger to make. "My father sends limousines to pick up all his guests, but I've always been ashamed to." An odd way of putting it, he thought. "Come the way I like best—I used to do it when I came home as a child. Get on the ferry to Mount Vernon."

"Where do I get off?"

"Leave that to me." He was happy to.

The Potomac was serene. He almost hated to see it disturbed by this clumsy chug of intruders and the blare of a loudspeaker. "Fort Washington is coming up on the left." But he was looking to the right, where Mount Vernon should be—he had never been there. Then he noticed a little motor launch drift off a near point of bank, kick a bit of water, and turn. As it came, it dug a witch's wake, all firecracker-popping of lights along the water.

Lynn was at the wheel. She waved at the captain and he ostentatiously walked to the other side. Others could look, but the captain never did. She swooped near, cut the motor, and drifted by. "Got any luggage?"

"No."

"Throw your book." She missed a one-handed catch, but batted it down into the boat. "Jump at my next pass."

She gunned the motor, made an arc, slowed, tilted so her slant of hull stood for a second almost parallel to the ferry's blunt side, and he jumped down quickly, afraid to look afraid. He did a lurching land, feet, knees, hands hitting so fast they seemed to touch down all at once. He clung to the far (dipped) gunwale, to keep from tumbling right over it.

"How did you ever make that jump as a child?"

"I did break my ankle once."

"Thanks for warning me."

"At Button's is more your speed, I guess." He agreed with her, but not as heartily as he would have a few months back.

She lifted the boat's nose. Water had wet her shorts and shirt, here and there, and made him remember what a lubricious word "lubricious" is. Her bare thighs were tan, and the fuzz on them tangled the sunlight. He squinted, and she handed him sunglasses. Her forearm, as she steered, was goosepimpled with evaporating spray. "The tide is turning." She had to shout through blowing hair.

"Tidelands," he said lamely.

"Yes. This part of America grew up breathing to ocean rhythms. It was more a watery than a horsey set back then. George Washington preferred slow barges to quick stallions."

"I guess that's why we don't care much for Washington any more."

"Speak for yourself." He lifted his eyebrows rather than shout a question up into the wind. Her words were blown back at him. "In a world of swaggering toughs, he was toughest without having to swagger. Remember, I grew up in Virginia."

The boat's nose nuzzled down to a berth she just touched, with a magic change of flying to wallowing, and he rocked his way over the gunwale as she tied up.

"You look wilted in that suit. Want a swim?"

"Sure." She took him straight through a hedge to the bathhouse. "There are trunks in there. I'll go to my room for a suit."

He changed and slipped into the deep end, tensing with the cold, a rigor vitae. When she came out of the house in her bikini his wet eyes gave irises to her melodic walk, to her browned skin and "brown hair over the mouth blown." She dove neatly and swam to him. The hair came up stringy and plastered over her face. It seemed to make her vulnerable; so, on an impulse, he kissed her She pushed her hair aside. Little chlorine fires were kindling in her eyes, and her mouth was set. She knocked his arm off the side of the pool, wrapped her legs around him, and clung to him with a kiss of clenched teeth on clenched teeth. He sank happily enough, just mildly wondering at her ferocity. It did not let up as he ran out of air, this rigor-mortis embrace. He tried to push up from the bottom, but her legs, lashing behind him, kicked his feet out from under him. He tried to free his arms, but her thin arms, pinning them, were strong, and her whippet body curled tighter. He finally got a hand on the pool side and started levering his way up with it; but just then she released him, swam to the end of the pool, and went inside.

He got out shaken, trying to laugh at his own panting. "Maybe she does CIA work on dolphins as weapons." But the desperation in that grip unsettled him. He dressed and walked by the pool, not wanting to enter the house, wondering what to do next. She solved that by coming out, brisk and toweled, as if nothing had happened, her hair and breasts lifting contrapuntally with each jaunty step. "Want to see the place?"

"Sure." She took him through winding hedges with glimpses of open grass. Black shadows velveted the inlaid greens of lawn. He was looking back when he found himself in the cool shade and heavy odors of a stable. "This was my favorite spot, growing up. We had more horses then." He saw two in the six stalls. "God, how I hated the term 'horsey set'—though I loved the horses. I made a bargain with the horses. I wouldn't talk about the embarrassing company we kept if they wouldn't."

They circled a greenhouse with covered embers of green and red foliage—she waved at the gardener through the milky panels—and went into the huge Georgian house by a back way. A broad hall gave onto rooms dark with furniture and glinting with silver, huge portraits of family members in heavy frames—he saw one of Lynn as an awkward teenager, but she pushed him quickly by it. "No paging the family album, please." In a library full of eighteenth-century bindings, she mixed drinks while he checked the books—about half looked authentic. "Fake or real," she said over her shoulder, "they're never read now, not even by me. But there are some Addison first editions that Harris still covets."

She went over to a window, and sat in its deep sill, tucking her legs under her. The sky was paling; it seemed to get clearer instead of darker at a hint of night. He pulled a large leather chair around to face her. "Was it Harris who brought us together, as he did in Cambridge?"

"Yes, that monster."

"What do you have against him?"

"For one thing, the way all you little boys play up to him."

"You want us to be as hostile as you are? It's easier for a woman to go around snatching his cigars."

"That's a boy's excuse, not a man's."

"What's this eternal-boy stuff—I don't act like a boy around him." (Just feel like one, he was thinking, as he protested too warmly.)

"Then why are you always apologizing for your crass commercial line of work?"

"Who says I am? Did he tell you?"

"That's another thing I don't like about him. He knows too much about everybody. It's creepy."

"He just likes gossip. It's a professor's trait."

"It's not the professor I hate."

"Then why do you go to Button's?"

She laughed: "To play Eve in your Eden." Then, serious, after a silence: "I think you know . . . I work for him." Then a wry grimace: "We're all Addisonians here."

"Except the Boswellians."

She looked quickly at him, not sure what he meant.

He took a chance: "Those engaged in the Boswell Business."

"Don't ever say those words again! Not ever in your life!"

Night was silvering in behind her. She sat in a quiet that augmented her. There seemed no way for him to pick up the conversation. Then she bounded down from the ledge and said, "Want supper?"

"Sure. Can I help?" She gave him a quizzical look and went out onto a patio fragrant with flowers he had never seen before. A table was set, and a butler was pouring water into crystals. He wondered how and when she had signaled the man. She pulled Skipwith through the bushes and out onto a large rock. Standing on it, one could just see the Potomac hazily wink in the twilight. Then she sat, and pulled him down beside her. "I used to read all day in this spot. The trees were lower then, you could see the river even sitting down. The gardener once caught me sunbathing naked, but he didn't tell on me. I think he hoped it would happen again, but I was more careful after that. My mother thought it was 'unhealthy' to be alone so much, doing nothing but reading. But she kept getting me books."

"The Shakespearean mother."

"Yes, she used to slip away from Daddy's boring parties to read in her room. That is just when I got interested in the parties—or rather in the men at them. I would sit there fascinated. They were very flattered, and called me bright. They should have known what fascinated me."

"What did?"

"Their emptiness. I thought, *these* are the men who rule the nation? And sometimes other nations—Daddy's place is a regular stop for visiting potentates."

"I can see why. Is he here tonight?"

"No. Of course not," she said brusquely. "I wouldn't have invited you on a day when he would be here."

"Ashamed to let him see me?"

"Quite the opposite." She was up and brushing off her shorts. They went back through the clingy trees to the table, where candles were lit.

The candles went from dim to vivid as night slipped down, and the wine made him more open in his curiosity about her. She dodged most questions, bridled at some, but generally laughed his queries away. He was a little piqued that she showed no reciprocating interest in his past or present. Something seemed to be worrying her. Only when the butler had brought the brandy and left them alone did she speak seriously, at first hesitantly: "I've got to ask you a favor . . ."

"Anything."

"Don't go to London. You'll be in the way."

"I told you you didn't have to see me," he said stiffly.

"They'll connect us anyway."

"Who?"

"Some of those people you are not supposed to talk about."

"Boswellians?"

"Sh!"

"I don't care. They could just as well connect us at Button's in Cambridge."

"No, the ones I mean are on the other side."

"Will you be in danger? Then I *am* going."

"Oh God!" she said, flinging down her napkin. "The world is full of evil men and idiot boys. You think this is some adventure out of Robert Louis Stevenson?" She was pacing the patio, her arms hugging the thin blouse as if the candles could not warm the moist night. As she brushed the candlelit green branches, she seemed to be moving through liquid sparks of anxiety, with electric urgency.

"I don't understand this. If you work for Harris, and he asks me to go, how can you override him? Why doesn't he tell me not to go?"

"You are not to mention this to him."

"Come on, he's bound to know the At Button's delegation showed up in half force."

"By then it will be too late."

"Too late for what? You have to give me more to go on."

"I don't have to do anything. But I'll tell you this. I'm leaving early. And if I find you're coming, I'll come straight home with some important matters uncompleted. If you muck around, you'll wreck it all." Her voice had been quivering with angry emphasis, and she stalked back into the house. He followed her, but she was not in the dining room, nor in the library beyond. He poured himself a Scotch at the sideboard and wondered what to do next. Soon the butler came and said, "There is a car for you when you are ready."

The uniformed driver asked if he had a hotel; if not, he could suggest one where Mr. Baker kept a suite for visitors. "No, take me to the airport." They bumped out a long dirt road and then went through the tangled green and white light created by overhead signs and other cars—past Washington, whose lit buildings had bloated again and looked dead.

x

He went to work on time the next morning, after three hours' sleep, since he felt a need to talk about his enigmatic day in Virginia. But Wingate came in late, and then brushed by him for an hour's conference with some technicians. It was noon before Wingate reached his office. Skipwith told him everything but the Boswellian part of the mission to London. A few questions showed that Wingate knew he was holding something back on him, but his advice was quick and definite. "I think she's squirrelly. I'd stay away from her. And speaking of squirrels, this is no time for you to be playing that At Button's game. I've just built a better squirrel cage, and the world will beat a path to my door if you can just slip my toy past the Old Man."

"What do you mean?"

"Let's go lunch in the park. I don't want to give away *too* much to the friendly office bug." He looked around as if he almost meant it.

On the way to their hot dogs, Wingate explained: "It's those exercise machines. We did a sample run on campuses, and found kids will buy even the geriatric running machines being manufactured now, if we put a few gadgets on them. Seems the kids are too lazy to go out and run around a track; but they'll run on a treadmill if you give them little mechanical rewards. It's just like training mice. I designed a machine that clicks every hundred yards, rings a bell at each mile, and at ten miles the damn thing has an orgasm—lights up like a pachinko machine in heat. The tough part has just been solved—fixing it so the machine can't be cheated. Every time you stop for more than ten seconds, the odometer goes back to zero. Those little mice have to *work* for their cheese." He seemed equally delighted by his own ingenuity and the buyers' idiocy.

"Your only fun seems to come from making people pay you to mock them."

"It's the only way to stay sane. Look at all those gentlemen bullshitters who *believe* they're improving the world with their brand of soap. And speaking of such idiots, I really need you on this one. The Wolfsons are going to faint dead away."

"Why? It sounds like you have enough to fake a market-analysis pitch."

"Yeah. But I stole the money to make the prototype."

"You *what*? You're the only person I know who would never let himself get mixed up in anything *totally* honest."

"Alley cats learn to live on garbage and get proud of their skill."

"How did you steal it?"

"I took the money that was supposed to develop new TV games. They'll shit all over me for a few days. But it'll pass if they think I'm about to make them several million dollars—and I am. We've just got to get this past the Old Man. He won't think it's crap if *you* call it pop art or something. You're our arbiter elegantiarum."

"My, what phrases crooks are using these days."

"Don't give me away. Even alley cats eavesdrop on learned couples in the sack." Beneath the banter Skipwith was uncomfortable. He didn't think it would be hard to find a way of approving this project. But he knew, and Wingate did, that Wingate had a favor owed him from the Llad encounter. Skipwith felt half-obliged to like the thing even if it *were* unworthy of the company.

Wingate seemed to sense his uneasiness. "Don't worry. It looks like a goddam spaceship. If we can get Andy Warhol to use it just once, they'll put it in the Museum of Modern Art. I think we'll finish it over the weekend. Then I'll roll it into the Monday sales meeting and sell it to them fast before they ask where the money came from. Are you with me?"

"Well, let me see it first."

"Good. You're with me."

"I hate to buy any idea of yours. I know what contempt you have for your customers."

"You're not a customer. You're a coconspirator." Skipwith realized he would have to think about that later. Someday Wingate was going to get the kind of idea that sends you to jail.

Not even Wingate's antics could distract Skipwith from that dinner in Virginia, the harassed, almost hunted tone of Lynn's voice. He remembered her fierce underwater hug, and bristled at the contempt in her voice when she talked of "idiot boys." But who were the "evil men" of her phrase?

Though she had told him not to call Harris, there was no one else he could talk to. He had called her in the morning and she would not come to the phone. Wingate had been no help— Skipwith could not tell him enough. He would wait till Harris got home from class; he might talk more freely there than at the office.

That night he plunged right in: "Lynn doesn't want me to go to London. She's leaving early, and says she'll come straight back at the slightest word of my arrival there."

"My, my, something must have got into her. Maybe she just doesn't like your company."

"I think there's more to it than that. She seems afraid of something."

"Oh dear, it's her trouble coming back. I should warn you, my boy, that she has had some bad episodes of mental care. I'll try to keep her home. There's no reason At Button's should attend *every* Enlightenment Congress. Unless you'd like to go alone?"

"That's all there is to it?"

"All I can think of."

"Oh. Sorry to have bothered you."

"You know it's always a pleasure to talk to you." They chatted a bit, Harris urging him to go to London alone, Skipwith backing off from the idea.

xi

Next day in the office he told Wingate. "Scratch all the puzzles about Lynn Baker. Apparently she's been in and out of mental homes. Perhaps that's why you heard of her."

"I don't think so. But that reminds me of something." He started to go out, but turned back: "Who told you this?"

"Harris."

"Still a believer, eh?"

"Why not?"

"We'll see."

Just as he was getting ready to leave for the evening, Wingate came back. "I owe you a favor, and this one took some doing."

"You don't owe me anything." Skipwith was hoping the exercise machine would cancel all debts between them.

"Not now. I remember where I heard of Lynn Baker. It was when I checked on student activists for the Agency during the sixties. She was suspected of leftist activities at her snooty college. I thought I could find more but didn't. It seems to have blown over. But this I can tell you for sure. She's never been in a mental institution. Your gentleman friend is bullshitting you."

"How do you know this?"

"Tricks of the trade. Friends. Alley Cats United."

Skipwith called Harris again that night. "I'm coming to see you."

"Always glad to have you. But why this suddenness?"

"I'll tell you there."

"I anticipate that with *very* great pleasure."

As the plane droned toward Madison, Skipwith felt as if he were inside a giant dentist's drill, drilling air, finding no tooth it could bite into. Every question brought answers that darkened instead of enlightening. When the tug of the plane slackened, he could not wait to hit the ground, to go after Harris. This time he would stay and ask till some answers at last could be leaned on without crumbling.

He loved the Wisconsin campus from his earlier visits with his father and Scott. They had always gone straight for Harris's office, and were passed in ahead of students clustering about it. The students were still there—which proved that some kids were interested in things other than exercise machines. Harris made most of those he dealt with get through all of Addison before they left the university.

Inside the big, roomy office, books were piled in front of bookshelves, almost to the ceiling. Harris often had to dismantle his library in order to use it. The Doberman pinscher was a fixture too, petted daily by the students. Skipwith remembered the room with fondness. He had found in it the cheerful and childish love of books he missed at his own college. But he didn't even glance around today. "What's this about Lynn being in mental homes?"

"I never said that, dear fellow. With her wealth, things were handled very discreetly. Specialists in the home. Money hushing up what money first caused, then had to cure. You know the kind of thing."

"Was she a communist of something in college?"

"Or something. A childish fling. Revolt against rich parents. Sophomoric leftism. It caused some problem in clearance for our work. But she was cleared, so you know it came to nothing. But why this flurry of semi-accusing questions, my friend?"

Skipwith felt ashamed of his own energetic aimlessness. He had nothing to follow up with. Harris smiled doubt away by his very manner. "It was just something Wingate said."

"*Not* a nice man, you know. I hope you have not let that little scuffle with Llad make you rely on him. I was speaking the truth when I said there is more to his past escapades than even the malicious have cared to suggest."

"Oh, he's all right. He likes scheming for its own sake. He's a person who will tell you ten lies so you won't believe him the eleventh time, when he's telling you a truth he doesn't want you to learn."

"One can see that pleasure becoming addictive, I admit. But it is a dangerous pleasure—dangerous for those around him. You are dear to us, Gregory. I hope you take care."

"I'm not afraid of Wingate."

"Others have made that mistaken boast, I feel obliged to warn you."

"What was behind that payola scandal? Wiretapping?"

"Oh, heavens no. He put that story around himself. He had several recording companies tearing their floors up and boring through walls. You can imagine the paranoia of wiretapping rumors in a place entirely made up of wires. I think that was the joke in Wingate's mind. But he got his information in the oldest way possible—sleeping it out of secretaries, one by one. Seriatim. Quite a performance."

"Well, you can't condemn a man for being a sexual athlete."

"Oh, not *that* so much. The real performance was the way he kept it quiet. I don't know what story he fed those girls, but the greatest gossips in the world, working in an industry that runs on gossip, never told on him. He has an odd gift for recruiting loyalty. Do you know what it is?"

"Something about flattering by insult?"

"Perhaps. Quite sinister, though."

"You said you had worse things on him than wiretapping. Now you tell me you didn't even have that."

"No, of course not. Minor matters, really. But one man was *not* charmed by Wingate, and was not going to keep quiet. Wingate killed him. An executive in the very firm he was supposed to be wiretapping."

"I can't believe that."

"It's true, though. Ask him. I wonder what story he'll come up with. Should be interesting. Let me know."

"How did he get away with it?"

"A number of people had to cover it up for their own reasons. It was called an accident—falling downstairs, struck his head, regrettable."

"He may have killed him by accident, in a fight."

"Oh, nothing so straightforward as that. You know he prefers the crooked path, the devious way?"

"He does that."

"Nice touch of humor in him too. Hobbling Llad in his own pants. I assure you Llad has not recovered from that little episode."

"I should think not. Why doesn't Llad turn him in?"

"He would if more serious matters were not involved. By the way, have you heard from Lynn again?"

"No, did you persuade her to stay home?"

"Fortunately, yes. Her troubles have never been more than a little rest and expert help could cure. She is impetuous, as you know. Remember my cigar?"

"Vividly."

"You should have seen her in my seminar. She fought like a tigress. And students fought to get in and watch her go at me."

"Did she know what she was talking about?"

"Absolutely."

"I'm surprised you put up with the hostility."

"You should know I like the best students. No fun doing all the testing, and never being tested. Will you stay the night at my place?"

He was tempted. It was a dazzling home, of Harris's own design, over a Wisconsin lake. He had stayed there once for a week when he came back from Korea in need of some guidance. Harris gave him the best advice when he sorely needed it. "No, I'd better get home."

"Please make it soon. There will be good fishing next month." Skipwith's father had fished there often.

"I'd like that," he lied. He was getting the stifled feeling of the schoolmaster's presence again. Harris filled this room with his easy certainty, just as he filled it with cigar smoke.

A thought occurred to him: "Llad won't be there, will he?"

"Oh dear, are you still holding that misunderstanding against him? It's not like you, Gregory. No, as a matter of fact, Llad will be gone most of this semester doing some work in Washington."

"Your work?"

"What do you *mean*, dear boy?" he laughed.

The flight back was stormy. The plane bucked and dropped hard as Lynn's boat had when it slapped its way over a wave. But then, with an eerie feeling, the plane slipped sideways, tricking the muscles that had tensed for buffetings against the head wind. The plane seemed to jolt loose again all the doubts Harris had narcotized. Skipwith wanted down, but not with the sense of mission he had felt over Madison. The plane tilted crazily on its approach, hit one wheel and jumped high, staggered for a grip on the runway. Skipwith was too involved with thought to be scared, but too scared to think to any purpose. He had been tossed free of all bearings. While others chattered, nervous with relief, he just sat there. He had nowhere to go. First he had lost the Weasel. Then Lynn. Now he was wondering if he ever really wanted to see Harris again. The haven of his life, At Button's, had messed up his life, he did not even quite know how. There was not that much life to mess up after Mary's loss. But what there was they had obscurely drained of meaning just when he felt life quickening again.

And Wingate. Was he a murderer? Why not? The world had broken loose and was lurching about insanely. What's one murderer more or less in the madhouse?

He didn't want to ask Wingate. But he had to, eventually, or stop working with him. Every moment he spent with him would be poisoned otherwise. But how does one ask another if he killed a man? Only one way.

xii

So the next morning his first words to Wingate were: "Did you ever kill a man?"

"Yes."

"In war, or something?"

"No."

"In self-defense?"

"No."

"Can you tell me why?"

"No. But who told you?"

"Harris."

"Ah, they're playing *rough*, aren't they?"

"What they?"

"He must have told you that, too."

"The CIA?"

"But I'm sure he told you not to blurt it out to others. You'd make a terrible spy, you know."

"You'd make a good one, if your own team could be persuaded to trust you."

"They couldn't."

"Is that why you left?"

"Maybe I thought my vaunted tapping and bugging skills would bring more on the open market."

"But Harris says you did not use any such skill in the payola matter."

"I didn't. But my feint had to be based on a truth in order to work. They knew I *could*, so they thought I *would*. Half the use of a skill is not having to use it." He was quiet a moment. Then: "Was Llad there while Harris was telling you this?"

"No. He is off in Washington, for some reason."

"*Is* he?" That seemed to interest him more than the accusation of murder. "And has Lynn called off her London trip?"

"Apparently."

"A strange world, my masters." At the door, he turned back: "See ya, Greg."

"Gregory."

"Yeah." But he didn't see Wingate for days.

In less than a week he heard from him. "You better come down here to Washington."

"Why?"

"Well, I may be a killer. But I think they're trying to kill your girl."

"What girl?" (Caroline had gone to California to live with a clothes buyer.)

"Don't play dumb. The Baker heiress you've been sappy for."

"Who? I mean—how . . . I mean: Where are you?"

"A motel in Alexandria. I'll pick you up at the airport."

xiii

Driving through rush-hour traffic from the airport, Wingate was surly and all but told Skipwith to shut up. "I've only got a few minutes to think how I'm going to play this. I've got an appointment with Llad in the bar of our motel. You go first to your room, give me ten minutes to prepare, then come down. Remember, we're here to sell the exercise machine franchise to an Alexandria manufacturer. The name of the firm is Solex, and the man we are seeing is Graham. Say nothing of Lynn Baker, even if I bring her up."

He drove with a furious concentration on something that was obviously not his driving. Skipwith's lurching mind went to appropriate rhythms.

"I'm late," Wingate said in the parking lot. "Check in. Be down by seven-thirty. The little bar off the dining room."

When he entered the dingy little bar, Skipwith expected to find the two men arguing—but not arguing, as they were, over Addison.

"I read him once," Wingate was saying. "I thought him a sissy—Hi, Greg, you remember Llad. If not, ask your Adam's apple."

Llad stood, shook hands, apologized for past misunderstandings. "Your friend is no friend to Addison. Too bad. He likes his own privacy, I daresay; and Addison went public with privacy. He almost took out a patent on it."

"Be careful," Skipwith laughed. "You're beginning to sound like Bonamy Dobrée."

"Dobrée!" Llad snorted at Harris's bête noire. "First *Victorian* indeed! Addison was the first Augustan. He made the Augustans august instead of disgusting. He taught those brutes to blush. Civilization was thought sissy stuff by the Tory bullies." Skipwith wondered if the cool Llad ever blushed. It would show in an instant on that milky blond skin.

"Are you in Alexandria on Addisonian business, Mr. Llad?" asked Wingate.

"In a way. We are discussing the composition of an At Button's delegation to the Enlightenment Congress. You may know Mr. Skipwith here turned down an invitation to be on it."

"Yes, but Harris told me no one was going now."

"We thought better of that." (You did so damn fast, Skipwith told himself.) "There are bound to be some people free who would enjoy the trip. Unfortunately, the congress does not come at an academic break this year."

"What do you folks do at these affairs?" Wingate asked. "Try to outpolite each other?"

"No. In fact, things get a little heated at times."

"Yes, we'll miss Morton now that he is gone," Skipwith broke in. Llad studied the remark to see if there was more in it.

Wingate continued: "What brings you to Alexandria? I don't remember any universities here with Addison scholars."

"There is a man in private residence here who is a Buttonite—Ed Higgins, you know, Gregory?"

"I know him slightly. Rich?"

"Very."

Wingate: "Think he might be interested in exercise machines?"

"At eighty?"

"Not for using, for investing."

"May I ask how you gentlemen knew I was in town?"

"Quite by chance. I was trying to get a room at your hotel, saw your name on the register. They were full, so we had to come here." Wingate read in his eyes the decision to check that story back at his hotel—he would find it false.

Llad was getting ready to rise. "Did you have something in mind when you invited me over?"

"Just wanted you to know we are in the neighborhood, in case you get a sudden urge to debate the authorship of particular *Spectators* in the middle of the night."

"Oh, very funny. But good to see you anyway—and especially to have the opportunity of apologizing to you, Gregory." He did it with grace and earnestness. Skipwith was impressed. Some of the Harris manner had rubbed off on Llad.

"Let's get out of here. I've got a lot to tell you and not much time," Wingate said. They walked through the crumbling grandeur of Alexandria's eighteenth-century port section, slipping down the steep cobblestone streets, avoiding strangers on the sidewalk, stopping by trees to let others pass in the dark. Wingate spoke in a hoarse voice less a whisper than reined-in command. "I've put together some of what's going on from old Agency ties. I still have some things they need. I better tell you now, since you're going to have to trust me tonight, that I killed that man for the Agency."

"You mean you were still with the CIA when you were with Freak Records?"

"Yeah, it was while the Agency was doing that silly runaround after the kids, trying to find Cubans peddling reefers after school, that kind of stuff. Only we *did* run across a man who was doing real spy work and using the record business as a cover. That's what puzzled us so long—he was not doing the things he *should* have been doing in that spot. He cared nothing at all about the radical young kids. He was in that for a buck. The nuclear patterns were kept entirely separate from the record business."

"If that's the case, the Agency can't expose you, as Harris threatened."

"They don't know how much loyalty I've got left. Besides, I did other things, several of them illegal, to cover up the murder of that agent. And I was compromised by the first attempts to get him to change sides. He was about to escape when others tried to capture him. They missed, and I had to kill him. They could get me just on the cover stuff—all that rigamarole about tapping and business espionage."

"Wouldn't they be afraid that you'd talk about the killing?"

"I might not be believed. I might also have an accident. Besides, as you see, they've not used it so far. I think it was just talk. But tonight could make a difference."

"Why?"

"What would you do if they tried to kill Lynn?"

"Try to kill them."

"I thought so. Even if she is a communist?"

"But she isn't."

"Actually, I think she is. Though I doubt that's why they want to kill her."

"Why do they?"

"Some double play. They don't want her to get to London. She's trying to get away, and has plane tickets in the morning. She's staying at a rich college friend's house here in Alexandria. I thought Llad might show up. And so, as you see, he has. They're clearly trying to stop her from going."

"But they told her to go in the first place."

"But she wouldn't take you. They suspect she'll try to bolt behind the Iron Curtain, and didn't want you suspected of complicity by the American police. Are you ready to shoot at your own government's men to save a Russian spy?"

"I'm ready to help her, any way I have to."

"Regular Galahad," he said mockingly.

"But why are you in this?"

"I like the game. I like to know who's playing and who's winning. There was damn little winning when I was there, I can tell you. You would almost think they were trying. I was forced out for trying to tell people that."

There was a light rain falling. "It could be a long night. You better take this." In the misty glitter the gun barrel looked liquid, but wasn't.

"I don't want that. What would I do with it? Shoot anyone who comes near Lynn?"

"Just take it. If the time for using it ever comes, you'll know. Wait upon the eloquence of events, as one of your eighteenth-century guys put it."

"Who?"

"Who cares? I just made it up. Your girl's in danger and you want me to check quotes?"

Wingate had come to a stop and was showing Skipwith how to let off the safety. He pointed to a Georgian home with elegantly carved white doorway. "That's her friend's house. Stay here." Wingate walked over to a dripping tree which seemed to move a little out to meet him—then Skipwith saw it was a man stepping part way from the shadow. Wingate came back.

"That's a private investigator friend of mine, great wiretapper. He's been watching Lynn. She's still inside. The only ways out of the house are the side door, the front door, and the garage. Watch them till it's time for her plane. There's a garden wall behind that can be climbed. My friend will cover that."

"Where will you be?"

"Watching Mr. Llad. His hotel is just a few blocks from here."

It was a long night, but hardly boring, as his mind raced and bounced about, trying to recreate each conversation with Lynn to see if it was conceivable that she was a counterspy. Do communists praise George Washington? If she was an agent, would she take chances for a man she had barely met? But of course, she was an agent, at least on one side, if not on two. Had her radical school days left her with a secret she had been hiding all this while?

He wanted to rush in and talk with her. But maybe that would put her in more danger. They would think he was scheming with her. Was the house being watched by *them*, too? Skipwith began seeing men under every tree. A cat moving out from one doorstep nearly made his breathing stop and it took an effort to start it again. The few passersby seemed to hurry or slow their footsteps in sinister ways. He was ludicrously glad the revolver was in his pocket, though he had sworn to himself not to use it. It just made him feel better, as Stevenson said the bull's-eye lanterns boys hid under their coats made them feel important—*they* knew they had a bull's-eye at their belly, though no light shone out. She had said that, hadn't she?—that he thought he was in a Stevenson adventure. Well now, by God, he was. He stood rigid in the spongy night, hearing hundreds of people talk fuzzily around him.

No one came in or went out of the house he watched melt into night and waver darkly through the rain. No lights shone from inside after one A.M. Lynn obviously had no packing to do. Her grips would come from her own home, or had been carried to the airport already. For hours he had seen only lighter black on black. Then first dawn, hardly visible, disturbed before defining the building's edges. His wait was not sweetened but soured by coming to an inconclusive end, a dribble of weak light and bleak inaction. He was happy to relax his ache of attention somewhat; but angry to be left still empty of conclusion. There was no eloquence to these events.

But just then the front door of the house burst open and a young woman ran out screaming, "No!" She was followed by an older man. Skipwith followed them, running through a mist that was half drizzle, clogging the lungs. They took one corner, two. Red emergency lights were pulsing regular, monotonous with menace, in front of a hotel. The two people he was following ran into the lobby, and he was about to run there when something hit him in the left side, where his rib had been broken. It drove him sideways, till he fell against a gutter. Wingate dragged him to a doorstep opposite the hotel. "She's dead," he panted.

"Let me go."

"Sure, run right in there with your gun and try to explain what brings you for a morning call."

"Take it. I never wanted it." He dug in his pocket for the gun. "Who did it? Llad?"

"Yes."

Skipwith struggled to get up; his rib felt as if it had been broken again.

"He's not there. He was gone when I got there."

"How did he do it?"

"Knife. You don't want to know."

"Was she dead when you found her?"

"Dying. She had one message for you. 'Kill Claudio.' You get it?"

"Yeah. Cymbeline became Beatrice before dying."

"Don't try it, pal. You're no Benedick. I told you not to go against Llad in a fair fight. Harris is far tougher. And I don't even know what his game is. He might be the good guy in this whole picture."

"Not if he killed her. How did she get out?"

"She must have climbed over the garden wall before you and I got there. She's in a room registered to a Sarah somebody. Llad must have told her to come for some reason."

"We've got to do something."

"Yeah. Sleep. You have any pills?"

"No." He tried to rise, and gave a little involuntary cry.

"What is it?"

"You broke my rib, you bastard."

"But saved your life."

"Don't bet on it."

Back at the hotel, Wingate took him to his room, gave him Scotch and sleeping pills. "You've been up all night. You're in no condition to think. I'll get a doctor's name from the desk."

"Forget it."

"You're crazy."

They told the doctor he had been mugged and that Wingate chased the mugger away. The doctor said it looked like he had

been shaved and bandaged there recently. "Yeah, I get
mugged a lot." Skipwith started to laugh and couldn't stop. It
was an ugly sound. The doctor saw the hysteria, gave him a
sedative, taped the rib, and told him to be at the hospital at
three o'clock for X-rays. "Now sleep."

After he left, Skipwith pretended to sleep, but Wingate
would not leave. Finally, he got up and went for the door.
Wingate blocked it. "Want to break my other rib?" Skipwith
asked. Wingate let him by, but followed him.

Skipwith had no place to go, and his rib was throbbing. Some
instinct forced him to *walk* out a meaning, though he could not
think. Walk *toward* meaning anyway. "Kill Claudio" recurred
to the broken rhythm of his steps, a distant cannon salute to her
passing. It was the first time he had really thought of killing
anyone. His daydreams of beating up Weasel One had been
just that—daydreaming. But this was a growing purpose,
something in his belly like a bull's-eye, or a gun; like a baby
formed and distinct and asking to be born. This he would be
delivered of. That alone was certain, in a tumble of indistinct
things.

Why? He had seen her only three times. Yet this hurt far
more than Mary's leaving. That had just ended his life. This
unthreaded the world's fabric. He saw again her profile in the
candlelight. It was like the air-drawing of light one sees after
closing one's eyes in sunglare. She had made the shadows
bright, and now she made this sunny Alexandria day swim in
darkness for him.

He was sweaty and trembling, from pain and sleeplessness,
as he trudged. But he kept threading and rethreading those
little streets with their big houses shabbily grand. He kept
summoning his Purpose to hold his stumbling walk together.
He felt again the power in her slim body as it curled around him
under water in that deathlike single kiss she had given him.
Rigor vitae. No tears. He must right his balance, steady his

walk, with the ballast of the hate he was carrying. Her face dazzled darkly at him. He saw again the green acetylene-leap of her glance.

Why was Harris Claudio? He didn't know why. But he knew. She had called Harris a monster, that day in her home, and it seemed the most improbable thing she had said. Now it was unquestionable. It was not a matter of argument, but faith—though like all faiths, his caught at rational hints or clues. Harris said she had broken with her leftist past. That had to be a lie. Harris sent Llad to do his killing. Skipwith would send no one. He would go himself.

His eyes were filled with salt water and he did not see a curb. The unexpected little step into air made him pitch forward into the street. Two passing ladies shook their heads at a man blind drunk on the concrete just after noon, and Wingate ran forward, but pulled back again when he saw Skipwith make it to his feet, look around in bewilderment—straight, for a second, at Wingate, though he did not recognize him.

Skipwith sought a cool place to collapse. A bar? No bars here. A church. He went in.

A noontime Mass was just finishing, and Skipwith hazily remembered morning Mass at the tony Anglican prep school he attended. His American parents believed in no God but England. His father must have thought, quite rightly, that he would come to believe in Addison rather than Anglicanism. But he had *half*-believed, some mornings—with the hymns and the high language pulling him back into history.

Nothing of that in this Roman service. This God had no style, Addison's or anyone else's. Good. God had no place in the same world with Harris. Leave Harris not to heaven. Leave him to Benedick. And why must Benedick do it? For the only reason left in a reasonless world. Beatrice told him to.

The Mass ended with a rustle of (mainly) women going out, their purses clattering. The priest came down a side aisle and

into a confessional almost at Skipwith's elbow. He heard the
buzz of elderly women's consciences, precise as their shopping
lists.

There had been a delayed Puseyite at his prep school, wearing his cassock all day like a socialist red tie, who tried to make
"his" boys go to confession. Skipwith admired the man's diction
and flair, and went once into his toy forgiving box. But only
once. There was something furtive about it all. It did not
cleanse, but dirtied. All right, he wanted to feel dirtied now,
readied for his task. Kill Claudio. That thought both steadied
and animated him, the headiest of brandies; he was getting
tipsy on it.

He started to laugh. Then feared he would not be able to
stop. Then stopped. Giddy and lightheaded, he stepped into
the confessional. "Father, I want to confess a murder."

"How many times did you commit the act?" Skipwith looked
up, and recoiled from the fuzziness of the priest's face—was he
going blind? Then he saw there was a gauze between them.

"How many times?" the priest repeated. It sounded hilari-
ous to Skipwith. He must ask that question, no matter what: I
confess to genocide. How many peoples did you exterminate?
He was beginning to giggle.

"Have you been drinking, my son?" The priest said it gently,
not in reproach.

"Yes," he laughed outright. "Brandy. The best there is."

"Compose yourself. Can I help you in some way?"

"Say it's all right. Or all wrong. Say something."

"Murder is always wrong."

"*There* ya go. But *you* don't know. This murder is going to be
fine. Finer than brandy."

"What murder?"

"Oh no, you can't trick me. You can't stop me. He's got to be
punished."

"He has wronged you?"

"Not me. Not even her. The world. His living wrongs the world."

"The world has often been wronged, and God has gone on forgiving."

"That's what's wrong. Forgiving is the sin. I don't forgive God. Not for him. Not for her."

"That *is* the hardest thing. Some find it hard to believe God forgives their sin. More, I'm afraid, find it hard to believe he forgives others. I think the hardest thing, in the end, is to believe we can forgive him."

"I *won't believe* that. It would insult him. I hate him, but I won't insult him."

"Would you insult the man you mean to kill?"

Skipwith had been wavering as he knelt on his little cushion, but he stopped to think of that. "No, I don't think I would." Then, with a giggle, "Just kill him."

"So you respect your foe, and God."

"God *is* my foe. Look at you. You sit here forgiving a lot of little people's little sins—and you don't even know if you can forgive God."

"Maybe it's the same thing."

"Great! That's all I need! A skeptic in the confessional! The world is not only crazy but crooked. Why can't you be honest and break out of this little box?"

"Step out in the street, like a man?" the priest said mockingly.

"Well, yes," Skipwith replied weakly, sobering a bit to his own foolishness.

"Taking the sword does not prove you are a man. You want to take the sword of vengeance now. Is there any way I can dissuade you? Did you come here to be dissuaded?"

"I don't wield this sword, Father. It wields me." He regretted his game, weary of it. He got up and had to find fresh air. But then his side seemed to tear open, and he slumped sidewise against a pew, tried to sit in it; slid to the floor. The marble was cool.

"Some killer," Wingate muttered, and moved to pick him up.

The priest had come out, and watched Wingate get Skipwith to his feet. "Take care of your friend," he said softly.

"Sure, Father."

xiv

When he woke in the hospital, the first thing he remembered was Wingate outside the hotel saying she was dead. The red emergency lights pulsed across his face like rapid blushes of her blood. Wingate was saying, "Kill Claudio."

The phrase played and replayed itself in his head, and he said it out loud a couple of times, in a matter-of-fact way. He had just said it again when Wingate entered. "Enough of that, Greg. You're not gonna kill anybody. What did that priest tell you?"

"What priest?" Wingate found out with a few questions that the message from Cymbeline/Beatrice was not only the first thing Skipwith remembered when regaining consciousness, but the last thing.

Skipwith was still working back from that moment in the red lights. "Did they get Llad?"

"No, they're looking for some lover she had last year and brushed off."

"When did she brush him off?" His jealousy was childish, but he didn't even try to hide it.

"I don't know."

A few days later Skipwith was back in the office, and Harris was trying to reach him on the phone. He would not take the calls. He had to talk to him. But in his own time, on his own terms. And not at a distance. He had an intention—he did not know where it came from, and did not question it. But he had no plan.

Wingate would not help him plan. He said, "I'm sorry I got you into such dangerous company. You didn't save the girl. That was all that mattered. Forget the rest. They'll fuck themselves up if it's the same old gang I knew. They've probably got the CIA watching you now."

"I don't think Harris wants any more people than necessary to know about this. You notice he risked sending Llad to get Lynn. Whatever his game is, it is not fucked up, and it doesn't seem to be run out of the Agency."

"You're learning. But not enough." He left; but came back daily trying to reason with Skipwith.

The next Tuesday he said, "I see you've asked for a few days off. Where you going?"

"Wisconsin."

"I thought so. Have you got a gun?"

"Yes." He knew Wingate would not help, and had got it on his own.

"I thought so. I could tell the Madison police and have you picked up."

"They can't keep me in jail forever."

"Harris is probably guarded. You'll never get at him."

"We'll see."

"Maybe I better go along to keep Llad on his good behavior."

"No. I don't want to implicate you in a murder."

"*Hold* to that fine thought! But why implicate yourself?"

"You heard her."

"Let me fly out with you. I deserve one last crack at bringing you back to your senses."

Wingate used again all the same arguments on their flight. Skipwith would probably not kill Harris, just go to jail for the attempt; wreck his own life for Llad's amusement; fuck up the fucking CIA's work even further, in ways he did not know;

perhaps even help some enemy country in his blundering way. Good arguments all. But Skipwith was not arguing today, thank you. Not any day, till it was done.

After landing and renting a car, Skipwith said, "You can do me one favor. I'm known at Harris's office. Just go look at the schedule posted on his door, find out what time he has class today. Meet me at the drugstore over there."

By eleven A.M. Wingate was back. Skipwith was drinking a soda. "Only one class today, at one this afternoon."

"I've got to leave now."

"Let me drive out with you. I won't go in. You're crazy enough to be Don Quixote, but I'm not colorful enough to be Sancho Panza."

It was not worth Skipwith's energy to argue. He was saving all his purpose for the encounter.

"I'll get into his house before he can get back from class. Stop here." Wingate had been driving while Skipwith checked the gun. "Do you want to take the car back? Or you can leave it here and hitch back. I don't care."

"I'll hitch." They had driven forty minutes into the hilly lake region of Wisconsin. Skipwith had directed Wingate to park by a beech grove. He didn't want Harris to see a car near his house when he came back from class. Skipwith moved so fast he was almost running through the grove. As Wingate watched, the blink of light through the beeches made him flicker like an old movie character.

It was Indian summer in Wisconsin, classes just back in session, the dairy country still unquickened. A frothy sky with white scrambled-egg clouds stood out over the clear lake; and the house jutted out over it from a high cliff at the water's edge. Harris could go down a rope ladder from his living room straight to his fishing boat.

Skipwith panted up the cliff—good, no car; circled an outside cooking area, with garage and tool shed, and tried the door of the house. It was open. Typical. Harris was famous for not locking up. His loyal students made sure no books or exams were stolen from his office. Skipwith nudged the door open and went for the living room. It was long, bright-lit on three windowed sides, with a smooth hardwood floor. Harris often held seminars there for his prize students, with a roaring fire at one end of the room.

"Welcome!" Harris roared from his little desk beside the fireplace. "Come right in! You are expected!"

"I thought this was your class time."

"Canceled in your honor! I heard from New York you were on your way."

Skipwith pulled his gun: "Were you expecting this?"

"But of course," he smiled.

"Drop it," came Llad's voice from behind. Skipwith turned slowly, saw a rifle leveled at him, and Harris's Doberman leashed beside Llad. He dropped the gun. The dog, on command, retrieved it.

"That will be all for now, Llad. I'm sure his prank is over." Llad took the dog into the anteroom, but left the door open.

"Did you kill her?"

"Well, now," puff, puff. "That depends"—puff—"on what . . ."

"Don't pull your cigar act on me. I want an answer."

"*Act*?" He was more shocked by that word than by an accusation of murder. Skipwith remembered how calm Wingate had been when accused. He was joining a cool club, these murderers.

"Yes, I suppose I killed her. But so, after all, did you."

"What . . . Where do you stand in this?"

"Ah, that is difficult to answer. I stand nowhere and everywhere."

"Stop riddling."

"You wanted an answer. All good answers are riddles. To tell you where I stand will take some time. I think you should sit."

"I'll stand."

"Ah, youth. I was young when the turn came that made me stand where I stand. Alone. That was during the war. I was in the OSS, you know. But I started in the infantry, on Guam. And I ran the first time I saw Japanese fire. My squad leader clubbed me down with his rifle. I lay there unconscious during the engagement, and woke wanting to die, a wish my fellows almost gave me. Their contempt baked off them. I could feel it even when they were not voicing it. It made me quite a little hero after that. Two islands later I was known as a fierce Jap hater. My 'colleagues' didn't realize that my hatred was not for 'the Japs,' but for them. When I went into the OSS, my joy was at showing how unintelligent are intelligence officers—not a difficult job; but one more subtly rewarding than knocking off Japs.

"I returned from war to an insipid wife and a teaching job that bored me. This is not boring you, is it?"

Skipwith was pacing back and forth before his desk, wanting to hurry him, but guessing the secret he wanted would be buried in this autobiographical ramble. Long as he had known Harris, he knew none of this.

"My life seemed so drab I began to toy with the idea of suicide. I found, to my delight, that the very toying with death made life interesting again. Perhaps you've had the feeling?"

"Go on."

"I even tried a few times, but I could not find the *absolutely* appropriate way. After a while the game became ludicrous by its lack of conclusiveness. I mean, the minute I suspected I wasn't really going through with it, the thrill was gone.

"I tried other ways to stimulate the same feeling. The thought of murder interested me. But murder put you at other people's mercy, a ridiculous price to pay. I mean, in order to control one person's destiny, you put *several* others in a position to control you.

"So I began to refine the methods of control over others. It is a game all teachers play, though not very well. And don't think only teachers play it. Employers do. Husbands and wives do. Parents play it cruelly, and best of all. Your friend Wingate is a master of it—look how he rubs in the dependence of that company on his brains and nerve, 'cutting off people's balls' as he puts it, and then laughing at them. Love and hate are indistinguishable so far as this great game is concerned. Look at the way lovers constantly test each other: 'How much are you willing to *sacrifice* for me, how much will you *put up with*?' Most infidelities are love-tests, a way of saying, 'If you really love me, you won't hold even *this* against me.' It's sickening."

"If the game is sickening, why do you play it?"

"It is sickening only because people do not know what they are up to. When they begin to suspect, they do not have the nerve to see. *Aude sapere*, you know. They lie to themselves in order to keep lying to each other. It makes one ashamed of one's own kind. Your little love had caught a glimpse of the truth. Did she tell you how she preferred the company of the horses to the horsey set she grew up in?"

"Yes."

"You see? I am different because I have gone all the way in knowledge, and then have used that knowledge. Others play the game ill, pretending not to play at all. I play it *very* well, while knowing just what the game is about. I made my first experiments somewhat clumsily, but I learned from them. That led to the little difficulties at Catton College, soon after the war."

"Yes, I heard of that."

"You heard it was a tenure fight over the lack of publication?"

"Something like that."

"You see, I was not so bad even at the outset. It was a sex scandal in those innocent times; but I made everyone so ashamed to talk of it that they could not let out even the small part of the truth they knew. For one thing, they thought I was a

participant in the sex business. But my game was to compromise others without getting compromised myself. I began
by overseeing people's games with each other—letting students steal exams for their friends, not themselves; knowing
just enough to let them know I was overlooking it.

"But I found that students in that bygone age were more
ashamed of sexual indiscretions than of anything else; so I came
to know and encourage the early experiments in group sex. It's
amazing what people will do rather than confess to a homosexual affair. Once they were in my power, I could put them up to
little games like obscene phone calls to the dean—always without incriminating myself. If anyone talked, I could say I knew
something but was trying to help the lad (or lass); I withheld
some knowledge, rather than destroy a promising career. Oh
yes, I had to have worthy adversaries. I always went for the
ones with promise. You are aware of my fabled influence over
students?"

"Of course."

"It is the influence of fear in most cases. They know what I
know. It is a wonder I have not been murdered—except, of
course, that they *were* bright enough to reject murder for the
same reason I did. Besides, in most cases, my only reward for
knowing *was*—knowing that *they* knew. I never blackmailed or
coerced. I steered and suggested. The outright blackmail, the
thing that pushes others to the wall, makes them panic—never.
It has no doubt saved my life a dozen times over."

"What did you have on her?"

"Ah yes, the pugnacious Lynn. It had to be something good
on her, didn't it? And it was. She came to graduate school at
Wisconsin in the 1960s, just when campus radicals were in-
dulging in disorders I could use. And I knew from one of my
former 'disciples' that she had secretly become a communist in
college—revolt against the parents, you know, very banal—oh,
I told you that before. The fifties were my golden opportunity.
My OSS ties made me an adviser to the CIA, then a recruiter,

then a full agent. I used the knowledge I gained to sway communists as well. I kept Lynn out of the openly radical activities, which drove her into more serious Party work underground.

"Do you know what the Boswell Business really is?" Skipwith was still pacing the long, polished floor, trying to cool his jumbled feelings. Steer, then aim. "Morton and Brown used the theory that Boswell stage-managed and artistically created Dr. Johnson as a code for their attempt to set up advisers to the CIA who would shape its policies in subtly self-defeating ways. The beauty of it was that Morton and Brown were communists in belief without having any ties at all with Russia or the Party or even mildly radical movements. Lynn was the only one who was ever a member of the Party, and I persuaded her to sever those ties when she came to Wisconsin. They see it as an act of noble spontaneity, relying on their own initiative and idealism. I see it as putting them all in my power, without tying me to anything treasonous or dangerous."

"But you let them go ahead with their plans?"

"Why not?"

"That makes you in effect a double agent."

"Hardly, my boy. You forget the beautiful simplicity behind all my complexity of maneuver. Compromise others without being compromised. I am a neutral. Imagine a man who races two great thoroughbreds, both of which he owns. He may favor this one or that one at times, but he is really above partisanship. He wins, whoever wins."

"But there is no one to put the winner's wreath on your horse."

"No, I long ago surmounted the vulgar gratification of having an audience. I am my audience. I make sense, to myself, of the world. I inject the one real bit of order it has in it."

"Where does Llad stand in this? Is he part of the Boswell Business?"

"He knows about it, of course. It has always made him a bit

nervous—as you found out in that regrettable alley. No, Llad has been admitted to my secrets—in proportion as I have laid away insurance that he will never use them against me. Actually, he has some of the appetite for the game that I have. I may make him my heir to the world, my promise that the mess will continue making sense even after my death."

"Now I know part of your secrets."

"Of course, dear boy, it's only fair to let you know why you must die. It's the civilized thing."

"Why did you never try to put me in your power?"

"I never felt I had to, till it was too late. You played a different role. Scott suspected something of what I was doing, but could not get a firm grip on the matter. He introduced me to you, as a man so ingenuous you would tell him if you came across something wrong. You did, in fact; but you didn't know it. It may damage some of the righteousness I seem to hear swelling in your silence if I tell you that you are the cause of Scott's death."

"It was a suicide."

"Yes, we arranged it well. You see, I gambled on your ingenuous qualities, too. You hide so little. We played a deadly game through you, and I must say he was worthy of my mettle."

"So I was a pawn being moved on your board."

"*Do* not think so *meanly* of yourself. You were a murky pane through which we traced each other's movements. Murky, but just transparent enough. It was better not to know or control you. That would destroy your usefulness as a window on the enemy. Actually, in recent days, I have toyed with the thought of controlling you rather than killing you. But I hadn't time to come up with much on you before you forced my hand—or Lynn forced it. I learned that you turned in your best high school friend for getting a girl pregnant, when she was keeping loyally silent. I don't know how much that troubles you."

It troubled him like hell—and had, all these years; he dreamed of the look of betrayal that girl had given him. But now he felt doubly shamed by the fact that Harris knew of that childish episode, and had thought of using it. A man who knew that might know anything about him, things he did not even know himself—like his part in Scott's death. No wonder Lynn hated Harris while working with him to serve her beliefs. He began to envy her, that life, that straight arrow-flight of hate, hate of the sort that was driving *him* now, yet calming him too.

Harris seemed to read Skipwith's thoughts. "And Lynn. You should have the satisfaction of knowing that you indirectly caused her death, too. She was the truest believer of my flock, true to her fierce and instinctive Marxism throughout. But she didn't want you to be caught up in our life. I sensed that, and was sending you to London with her, to compromise her with the thought of your being compromised. To prevent that, she planned to leave early and defect to Moscow. It could have led to trouble for all the Boswellians and some Addisonians. It was hard to lose her. She would never have risked us for herself. It came as a great disappointment to learn she would risk us for you."

Skipwith turned away, trying to be alone for a second with this terrible comfort. Her life had not been a straight arrow-flight of hate after all. It had wavered, because of him. And that wavering suddenly turned him weak. He had walked to the door of the anteroom, and turned back to look all along that hardwood surface at Harris's hard smile. He was lighting a cigar, efficiently this time. Skipwith moved toward him, but with a new numbness, a lethargy of agnosticism about everything, even the validating anger. He managed to keep moving; but it was like splintering down through floor after floor of a rotten house. And each room he dropped down into was the same room, with Harris sitting at the end of it. He moved quietly through this noise of wreckage, the silence getting louder and louder, till Harris snapped it with a quiet word: "Thunder."

The accent was on the second syllable. Skipwith heard the

click of the dog's nails on the polished floor and turned to see Llad smiling. He jumped aside from the blur of slippery dog trying to get footing for his leap. Thunder slid by with a comic wrath, scrambling to reverse direction. Just as he was getting set to come at Skipwith from the desk, Skipwith shot past *him*, jumped up on the desk and leaped over a cowering Harris. He barely made the sill of that window with the rope ladder; teetering there, hoping the boat was not below; saw it was, but had to jump anyway, *feeling* the shot from Llad he had not *heard* yet, but feeling it as a vague presence only. He thought he could clear the boat, and twisted in air to protect his taped left rib. He was thinking so hard of his task that he did not feel his right arm go numb till he heard the sick thud of it on the gunwale.

The cold lake grabbed air out of him, but his feet touched ooze. He automatically trod toward land. The motor was not on the boat; it was useless. He splashed under the house's stilts, looking for a weapon.

Paint cans, rope, and oars. The motor. Nothing useful. Garden tools, he remembered, were in the shed by the cooking area. He picked up a rusty ice skate, the only pointed thing he could see.

The dog was out and barking on the patio, to Skipwith's right. He took an empty tin garbage pail, hurled it with his good arm (tearing his bad rib) toward the cliff on his left, and ducked toward the path for the beech grove while the dog noisily circled the house toward the garbage can.

Skipwith was running painfully, but he reached the grove. He was almost halfway to the car when he heard the dog's pants behind him. He turned to look and to draw a deeper breath. The dog moved smoothly, striped by the dim-bright of the beech shade hitting him, like a neon sign outside a Greyhound station. Skipwith turned to run, while looking for a stick. He stumbled and almost fell on the skate.

Trying to remember what he had heard while watching dogs fight (they go for the belly, that's why they belly-up to surrender), he worked his useless right arm up with his left hand, holding the skate. The right arm was so numb he did not feel the teeth sink in; which let him concentrate on digging the skate up into the dog's groin, using it as a lever to *throw* the thing over his own fallen body. As its shadow passed, blocking the light, his face and shirt went suddenly warm with blood. The pain in his rib made him think, for a flash, that the blood had spurted from his chest rather than the dog's belly.

The dog's momentum and the sweep of the skate carried it over his head, carrying his arm with it. But the dog let go of his arm with a howl, and writhed into a wormlike curl.

Skipwith got to his feet, still too excited to feel pain. He wished he had the gun still, to put the dog out of its howling. He turned to limp toward the car, but Llad said softly, "Enough." He was right behind him on the path now, and was bringing the rifle up. "I should have done this long ago. But Harris wouldn't let me."

A vague rustle and snapping to Llad's left made him turn, and there on the cliff was Wingate. The rifle swung and fired, wide; but Wingate went down in a comic genuflection, trying to steady his pistol. Llad took aim with the rifle, too slowly; as he posed, Wingate fired twice through his chest.

When Skipwith rushed over to him Wingate's shin seemed to bend slightly as it dangled in water. The bullet must have snapped the bone. Wingate was already fumbling with a handkerchief and a stick to make a tourniquet. Skipwith gave him his own handkerchief, to complete the circuit. "How are you?"

"I'll live. Don't let *him*." He jerked his head toward the house. "Take my gun and Llad's rifle."

He limped over to Llad, whose light skin looked blanched as the beech bark and chips he had fallen in. Dead peelings.

It was hard getting up the cliff, but he had to come in from high ground, run through the cover of the cooking area, or Harris could pick him off from a window before he got there.

The anteroom was empty; and when Skipwith eased his view around the doorway he saw Harris still seated at the desk.

"Is that Llad's blood or yours?" he asked. Skipwith realized only then how he must look, his hair and shirt clotted with blood.

"Your dog's."

"And Llad?"

"He's not bleeding any more." Harris sighed, rose; came partly round the desk, his hands empty: "The wise man knows the game is not always to the wise. You *may* have won. I'm not sure. You've already become something of a killer, like Wingate. In time you may rise to resemble me. Yes, I think you would have made a better understudy to my kingdom than the loyal Llad—perhaps overloyal. You may inherit yet. I comfort myself with that thought." He laughed as he stepped tranquilly over the windowsill.

It was only one window over from the one Skipwith had jumped out. But this one opened on rocks at the edge of the water. When he went to look, Harris's limbs were flung in a clumsy starfish shape.

Skipwith threw down the rifle. He pulled out the pistol at his belt and threw it over the lake he had fished so many times. "Pollution," he thought inconsequently. All Skipwith's nests were fouled. He wondered if the rest of the world was, too. He turned back. Not to Continent. Not to more Carolines. Then where?

3

Back at Button's:
New Orleans, 1977

i

SKIPWITH FINISHED TELLING MARCIA WHAT HAD HAPPENED "at Button's" in a hamburger-joint-cum-bar on Broadway. She sat there, frightened by his look, regretting what she had done. But she could not resist the temptation to ask: "You loved her, from those few glimpses?"

"I loved—some possibility that went out of life with her. I had seen one door close with my wife. I knew this was the last door closing."

"Yet what freedom could she offer, herself under communist discipline?"

"No one ever disciplined her."

"Then you could not have, either."

"I didn't want to."

"You make her more than human. No one can compete with that."

"No one would want to try. You wouldn't volunteer, would you?" he asked flippantly.

"No," she said, too quick. "I mean life itself can't compete. What makes you think everyone's shared reality should cut itself to fit your precise fantasy?"

"I've got nothing aginst life. I can take it or leave it alone."

"But you can't leave others alone. Look at all those you bumped around on Fifth Avenue."

He looked at her in surprise. He had not heard their cursing. "You bump into a lot of people without noticing." Her eyes had teared sympathetically several times when he was telling his story. They did so again; but this time he noticed.

"Oh-oh. I haven't bumped into you, have I?" She didn't answer. With a pound on the table, he shouted, "*God damn you, Wingate!*" The man at the hamburger grill moved out toward the door, ready to call a cop if he had to. Marcia put her hand over Skipwith's mouth as he muttered, "Damn him! Damn!"

He left her outside the shop, said he needed to be alone, and wandered off looking both dazed and determined. The next day she called him at the library, at his apartment. He wasn't there. She called Wingate, told him what had happened, asked if she should notify the police. "Don't," he said, "I'll find him."

"I don't think he wants you to."

"Then he won't know I have."

She heard no more for a week. Then her phone rang and Skipwith said, "I've got our tickets for New Orleans. Ben's going with us."

"Where have you been?"

"I'm afraid I was on a little drunk. Ben had someone get me to a motel and sober me up. I didn't know who this stranger was, but when I asked for Ben, the stranger went to a room three doors up and brought him in."

"You sure you want to go with him?"

"Yes. Get it over with," he said grimly. She shook her head at the repetition of his phrase from the day he disappeared.

"I can't go with you."

"Can't or don't want to?"

"Both. How would I get away?"

"You can always get away. It's getting back that poses problems." He said it with an air of resolution that made her want to see him going back. But she resisted.

"I told you I wouldn't go now."

"Yes, but that was a hundred years ago. I've been around the world since then. Welcome me back."

"You're crazy."

"I know. Be crazy with me."

"I can't. And you're still drunk."

"Then why is my head rolling around on the floor? When I was drunk it floated. Let me come over and persuade you."

"No."

"See you in fifteen minutes. I'll bring champagne."

"What are you celebrating?"

"Nothing. It's hangover cure."

He showed up looking terrible, hollow-eyed and trembly. He rattled the bottles of stout as he took them from a paper bag.

"You look like you need a lot of cure."

"Yeah. Someone told me half stout and half champagne will do the trick."

"Sounds awful."

"Nice name though—black velvet."

He tried, but gagged on the second swallow. "It's terrible."

She tasted cautiously. "I think I like it."

"And just when I was getting to admire you." He sipped champagne straight from the bottle.

"What makes you look so bad and sound so happy?"

"Resurrection. Takes it out of one, y'know. I bet Lazarus never recovered from his recovery."

"What were you resurrected from?"

"Life."

"Great. I thought you looked dead."

"I mean *my* life. I kept dragging it around with me. I was dead from all that weight of life with Mary."

"Who's Mary?"

"Never heard of her."

"Your wife?"

"Was. Who *was* Mary?"

"Is she dead?"

"For me. At last. I don't know if she's dead. I only know I'm not."

"You don't know, or you don't care to know?"

"Don't care to care. I thought I failed her, so I spent all my time trying to convince myself that she failed me. But we really had no project to fail on."

"You riddle too much."

"That's it. Backed myself into my cozy riddling corner, sat there on life trying to make it hatch some Meaning. A Meaning would pop out and chirp all the answers. You sprang me from my corner, you know. I hated you for it, one long night. I tried to run for cover, but I couldn't find my safe corner anymore." He mimicked Charles Laughton as Quasimodo, limping for a corner: "Sawng-chooarry! Sawng-chooarry!"

"Where did you go?"

"I'm not sure of all the places. But I made it back to our old neighborhood." He seemed to get sober as he drank more wine. "Our old house was for sale. I knew a basement window I could open when we forgot our key. It was still the weak link—made me feel downright affectionate toward it. I scrambled in, and scared a rat about half as much as it scared me.

"I thought I could never walk around that house again. It would mean too much. But it meant nothing. I had finally outlasted meaning. It wasn't there. I ran up and down the stairs. I practically skipped on the bare floors. I even sang a bit of *Fin ch'han dal vino*—though I wasn't on vino then. It was so easy. Why hadn't I done it before?"

"You weren't drunk enough."

"No. You did it, not the booze. You and crazy old Wingate. What a joke that he saved me twice, the second time just by being obnoxious. At first, mind you, I was afraid to open doors in the house. I thought I could hear whispers behind them, mocking me, all my plans, for me, for us; my great writing projects, her great admiration—neither forthcoming. I thought the least I would find would be our unborn children. God, I even had elaborate plans for them. I thought I owned them, and they hadn't even been born.

"I heard some mice or something in the walls, a kind of silly half-life to the house, and realized I had nursed nonmemories, memories of not loving."

"Drunken epiphanies. My street girls get them all the time."

"I know. But I *woke up* with this epiphany. You know, through all the drunken moods, the drag and lift of my jumbled chemistry, I kept thinking of your stupid work on the streets."

She laughed and looked hurt at the same time.

"You never took my dissertation seriously."

He paused, as if trying to find a way to deny it with honesty: "I took your seriousness seriously. I got boozily eloquent and earnest about your earnestness, and *untrapped* air. That study of whores was crazy and dangerous; but how your danger radiated life in the Brasserie that night we met. You were studying deaths in a riot of life."

"You make me sound like a vampire."

"Right! Right!" He was up now, swinging the champagne bottle. "You took your life out of their death the way artists drain off and redeem. Dickens in the debtors' prison. Hogarth in the Fleet."

"A doctoral thesis is no work of art."

"*Living* is your art. You've got the knack of it. How I envy you."

"What is this knack? I never noticed it."

"You wouldn't, that's part of the knack." He stopped in mid-pour and semi-pirouette, doing an unconscious parody of the stumped professor. Slowly he came back to earth, counting invisible things with his right index finger (the hand that held the bottle), neatly touching a whole row of nonexistents. "It *all* . . . I think . . . comes *down* . . . to *this*." He sat abruptly across from her, lining up airy pieces on the coffee table in a chess game of pure analysis. "*You* know life's coming around the corner." He turned suddenly, looking over his shoulder. "Or through the door. Or running with the mice in the basements and walls."

He turned back and winked. "But you're ready for it. You've got your own steam up already. Momentum, by God. All the best coaches tell their teams it's only a matter of momentum. You take life by surprise. You *up-end* the bastard before he knows what to do with you."

"And then?" She was laughing at the show she had become.

"And then? You look around to see what goodies life has spilled." He mimicked pawings at a bargain counter. "You see what you like . . ." He seized up all the pieces in the invisible chess game, and rose. "*Then you run like hell.*" He turned so fast he tangled his feet in his chair, and fell over with it rolling on him like a live thing.

She ran over, troubled and laughing, and kissed his returning laughter. "You know what I'm doing?" she asked.

He shook his head no, and winced at the blood-beat in that head, warning him while it inflamed him.

"I'm grabbing what I like." She repeated his bargain-counter gestures all over him. He laughed his way into her darkness, pleasantly drowning. Cured, after all, by black velvet.

In the morning, she said, "I'll have to run out and get some more summer dresses for New Orleans."

ii

On the plane, Wingate and Skipwith bantered, teased Marcia, schemed over Slatkin. Skipwith seemed younger to Marcia, more animated, almost boyish.

"You've never been to New Orleans?" Wingate asked her.

"No."

"You'll like it. It's a bighearted mudpie of a place. The kind local folk even built a hill in Audubon Park just so kids would know what one looks like."

"It's that flat?"

"The whole place is below sea level; it just slops around in the mush where the Mississippi ought to be. The muck is too gooey to bury the dead in, so they play musical coffins, shoveling the remains of corpses into a bin at the back of mausoleums when it's time to pop fresh bodies in at the front."

"Why don't they just cremate their dead?"

"Catholic place. Can't do that. The church would disapprove."

"But I always hear about its wide-open swinging life."

"As at Mardi Gras? Catholic feast. Lent gives an excuse. There's no corruption like Catholic corruption. It's hard to go to the devil in really stylish ways if you don't believe in the devil."

"Sure," Skipwith added. "That's what makes Graham Greene so good at describing seedy places—they are always *Catholic* outposts, nodes of awareness, in Mexico or Saigon or the Congo. There's a temperament that rides easily only in rot, like one of those boats that skims over the Everglades."

Wingate: "We better not give all the credit to the Catholic church. Think of the fear and protestant hatred Mark Twain floated through on the Mississippi. All that local color comes accumulating as a sludge and gets deposited downriver. The

colors overlap and cancel each other and turn black by the time
they get to New Orleans."

"Oh, I get it," she laughed. "It's the black hole of the
continent, sucking everything else in."

Wingate smiled back: "Yeah—the continent's cunt, that's
New Orleans." Skipwith looked puzzled.

"Where do you live, Ben?"

"In the Quarter. I have room for you both—even separate
rooms, if you insist."

"We insist," Marcia said primly.

"Where's the meeting to be held?"

"At Slatkin's home. He bought one of the old sugar planta-
tions up the Mississippi, kept the shell of the manor house, but
hired an architect to ream it out and hang a jumble of floors and
nooks and waterfalls inside. He has a fleet of limousines that
runs people in and out of New Orleans, but for the meeting he
has chartered a paddlewheel to take us up to his landing."

"It's nice to know the rich."

"I hope so," Wingate said fervently.

"Just what is your hustle with him?"

"Hustle? How dare you? I'm just pursuing a line of work you
got me into."

"What's that?"

"You gave my name to some student of conspiracies in the
New York reading room. She had theories on Elizabethan plots
she wanted to try out on me. I answered her briefly but civilly.
Soon I was getting letters from all over the country. These
people have a network of the most devoted researchers—
hundreds of them working at it full time, thousands doing
part-time work. Most do it at their own expense, though some
have backers. And I have the biggest backer of all."

"Really? Slatkin?" Wingate nodded. "That's odd. I always
thought him sane, though eccentric—of course, I only saw him
at our meetings."

"Half of him is sane, the business half. That's why I need a few members of the club to convince him I *do* know my stuff, about the Elizabethan period at least. I'm no scholar, so I can't get normal credentials from a university. But he knows and trusts two of the At Button's people, Jack Lewis and you."

"Well, what's the fuss about? I know you know your stuff—at least, I know you know more than I do, for whatever that's worth. I could tell that to Slatkin on the phone or in a letter."

"I told you he's a hard bargainer when it comes to business. He says he never seals a big deal without talking to the responsible people first."

"I don't like the sound of that."

"Why?"

"It means you are getting into him for a large sum, and you're making me partly responsible."

"Not for what I deliver. Just for what I'm bringing to the bargain, my knowledge."

"I'd never deny that."

"That's all you have to go warrant for. Slatkin wants to see you and Lewis together, in the At Button's context. I think he feels you would not lie where the Sainted Joseph might be called a kind of witness to the transaction."

"I should tell you," Skipwith leaned toward Marcia, "that Slatkin owns the best collection of Addison first editions and memorabilia in America."

"Yeah, he has a humidity-controlled glass cage, right in the middle of his house, to hold it. You have to walk to it from a low balcony, over a little bridge. The door raises and lowers itself by electric eye to keep the books from Mississippi rot. Addison's books get better treatment than our local corpses."

Marcia said she wanted to see the house, even though she couldn't go to the meeting.

"I'll take you there later to lunch," Wingate assured her. "In fact, how would you like to become a research assistant on the conspiracy project? I'm going to set up a library on his grounds. He trusts his own security people more than the New Orleans police. And I have to admit he's got a point there."

"What needs such guarding?" Skipwith asked.

"Testimony. I've already collected about a thousand hours on film."

"Sounds like you've already got approval for your project."

"Just the penny-ante part. I've got along with two or three assistants so far. Things will really begin to happen after our meeting. The foundation I'm going to set up will rank with all but the blockbusters of private foundations."

"But they're tax exempt. How are you going to keep politics out of the assassination theories?"

"This isn't politics. It's history. We'll be less identifiably rightwing than the American Enterprise Institute, less identifiably leftwing than the Institute for Policy Studies. We won't look for any one explanation, to fit one ideology. Any scholars with evidence will be welcome."

"But you used to tell me the conspiratorialists are all crazy."

"I did? Oh yes, I suppose I did. Did you believe me then?"

"Yes."

"Then believe me now. I know more."

"Why did you believe him in the past?" Marcia asked.

"Because his arguments made sense."

"What were they?"

"Ask him."

"No," said Wingate, "we converts cannot recite our old heresies. You tell her." He sat back and smiled through Skipwith's efforts to remember conversations held years ago.

"I can't remember all, or even most, of the things you said. I do remember what impressed me at the time. I had thought it was all too neat, too pat, things worked too well for a lone loony to have killed President Kennedy. You answered that the loony is the one most likely to succeed. Authorities have no way of anticipating his moves. He has no concerted plans to go wrong, no accomplices to gum things up, give things away, or talk afterwards."

Marcia was frowning. "But Oswald was traced, and did have plans. The FBI knew about him, and knew he was dangerous."

"They know about a lot of people, that they're dangerous. But to whom? Oswald tried to kill General Walker, planned to kill Nixon, and did kill Kennedy. What's the connection between the three? Why couldn't it have been any three other prominent political types—rightwing, leftwing, what have you? And things didn't work out neatly for him. He failed twice, and only succeeded because accident sent Kennedy under a window. When Oswald got his job, there was no way he could know that was coming.

"Or take Sirhan. Nobody knew—not Bobby Kennedy himself, or anyone on his staff—that he was going out of the hotel ballroom through that kitchen. He went, by chance, where a man had a gun and was ready to use it on any symbol of the world he felt was oppressing him. Arthur Bremer stalked Nixon and missed him. He even missed his chance with Wallace on one earlier occasion."

Marcia seemed unconvinced, and Wingate supremely uninterested. She asked: "How could Oswald shoot so fast and so well, from so far, and do all that by himself?"

"He didn't shoot well. Bremer sprayed bullets all through Wallace, and Wallace lived. Like Sirhan, he aimed for the heart. So did Oswald. The farther off Kennedy was, the harder target his head was to hit. He shot for the heart—from above, Kennedy's torso was exposed. But the gun fired high. One bullet went over his head, another—nonlethal—came closest, but went through his neck. The third, an inch or two higher, would have missed him, and he would have lived. It's a freak of chance, like Bremer's *failure* to kill Wallace under much better conditions."

"But isn't it odd that important people keep coming across these lethal nuts?"

"Only odd if you think there are just a few of them. But how can you think that? Imagine what the hate mail to Ted Kennedy reveals, every day, about this society. Consider how many guns there are in this country, floating around. And how Americans are brought up to think the ultimate vindication of a wronged individual is some shoot-out, just him against the system. Don't you realize the NRA says preservation of our freedom means the keeping of that option open? Take away the individual's gun and he is a slave, unable to shoot down Evil embodied in some other individual. In whom would such embodiment take place but the politicians and men of power?"

Marcia turned in confusion to Wingate.

"What's the matter with those arguments?"

"Nothing. They were good when I voiced them, and they're still good. In fact, I agree with all of them."

"Yet . . ."

"As a priori statements of the likely, they are unassailable. The trouble with conspiratorialists is that they took something that was emotionally unacceptable and equated that with its being psychologically unlikely. But the lone-nut approach is, as Gregory states it, far the likeliest explanation—so likely that it would take very hard evidence to convince me that this kind of assassination can be successfully planned and executed, and the planners go undetected."

"You mean you have that kind of evidence?" Gregory asked.

"I have the beginnings. But, first, look where prior conspiratorialists have gone wrong. They started with the hunch that three totally different lone nuts could not have killed the two Kennedys and Martin Luther King. Then they went through the Warren Commission volumes looking for things to confirm that hunch. Have you ever looked at those books?— not the report, the twenty-six volumes of testimony?" Both shook their heads no.

"It's a garbage flow, like the Mississippi coming into New Orleans. Every kook in Christendom came trotting in to tell his or her story to the commission. They were all treated politely and their gibberish was printed up, given that magic authority the printed word has for some people. The report does not bother to refute all the nuts, though the FBI checked out all their stories. So the conspiratorialists, who call the report ideologically motivated, take as gospel anything wild in the testimony that might throw doubt on the report. They trust the commission to print cock-and-bull stories accurately, and then treat eyewitness accounts as automatically trustworthy because they are set down in black and white. The conspiratorialists affect an objective scholarship, know all the 'sources' as if they were studying records from some dead Egyptian kingdom. But few have actually gauged the weight of each witness's testimony by investigating that witness and giving him polygraph tests. I'm not only doing that. I'm operating on the assumption that lone nuts did the killings and that half the witnesses I hunt down are lone nuts of a different sort. If those assumptions can be shaken by hard evidence, fitting no thesis, then and only then will I be convinced."

"Well, can the assumptions be impeached?"

"Yes. I've already done it."

"How?"

"I'll have to show you some of my material. I don't know who arranged the Dallas assassination. But I know how it was done. And no other conspiratorialist has even a glimmer of the truth."

"Have you given your findings to Slatkin?"

"No, he would charge around with them like a mad elephant, trampling what chance I have to find trails. That's part of the problem you're here to solve for me. I have to give him enough to show I'm onto something solid. But I have to keep him from knowing what it is until the time comes when it's safe to print—or to give our work to the Justice Department."

"It sounds like your only hope of succeeding would put your

foundation out of work."

"No, these are not things that will disappear for a long time, not in this generation or maybe beyond it. Grant the headiest vision of success and what do you have? An indictment or two. Trials of incredible length and complexity, historical doubts left unresolved, leads that fall short of indictment in one or more of the assassinations. Trials never solve historical puzzles. They are restricted to the guilt of the indicted individuals. To prove someone guilty, prosecutors must often surrender any hope of establishing other things. Take Jack Ruby's trial. To prove him guilty, the prosecutors had to omit things that would involve others. Trials are instruments for conviction, not investigation. That is why Oswald's death was not so important, from an investigative standpoint. He could have gone to trial and been convicted without answering any of the important major questions—just as Sirhan did, and Bremer, and James Earl Ray."

Marcia didn't want theory. She wanted to know what Wingate's evidence was. But he put her off with jokes, and talked the rest of the way about New Orleans.

iii

Wingate took them first to his apartment—on Dumaine Street. Cut into the sidewalk in front of the house—put there when the concrete was laid—were the words, "I dig pheasant doo." Wingate had to move a garbage pail to show it to them. "That's what endeared the place to me." The first floor housed a coin laundry, where two teenagers in Mother Hubbard dresses were stuffing a machine. Upstairs, in air-conditioned rooms with high ceilings, Wingate showed them the two bedrooms. "I'll sleep here on the sofa." Gregory said he would feel better not putting Ben out of his own room. "No, the phone is here anyway, and I may want to go out at night. My informants talk better at their own weird hours."

"I know about that," Marcia nodded.

"Wait a minute," Skipwith said. "I just remembered we need dinner dress for tonight. Can I rent at such short notice?"

"Of course, where do you think you are? Mardi Gras town has costumes more scary, even, than a tuxedo. But you might have to say you're going somewhere as Dracula to get one. We'll go right now. Come along, Marcia, and get a glimpse of the Quarter." As they headed up Chartres Street, he said, "I rented here because so many street kids end up in this part of the Quarter. Most are fascinated by conspiracy theories, and they do legwork for me at scandalously low pay. That was before I had tapped Slatkin's wallet."

After the men were measured for evening wear, they went up Royal Street and down Bourbon while the clothes were being assembled.

"Like it?" Wingate asked Marcia as a young man in denim shorts went by weeping profusely over a plaster doll in his arms, moaning, "She's dead, she's dead."

"I love it."

"So did Marina Oswald. She kept pestering Lee to take her into the girly shows, but he was shocked and disapproving. When's the last time you heard about an assassin who was also a letch?"

Skipwith: "Our new Caesars should say, 'Give me horny men about me'?"

"I say that already, and I'm not even Caesar."

"It's still early afternoon," Marcia said, "and this place reminds me of the carnival midway back in Ohio. The part where Mama wouldn't let us go. But look at the mothers here with strollers for their infants."

"That's the real secret of Bourbon Street. You've got sleazier or classier sex strips, but you haven't got any place where the most outrageous and the most respectable types mingle so easily together. Here shacks stand by the best restaurants, limousines are parked in front of dumps. Old and young, black and white, straight and gay, rich and poor—the place is catholic with a small c, despite the best efforts of Catholic bishops with a big, big C."

They came into the cruel sun of Jackson Square. Artists were sketching tourists in every shaded patch. "Why," Marcia asked, "do the artists display all these sketches of movie stars?"

Skipwith: "I suppose because they want to show they can strike off a likeness of some face everybody will recognize."

"It's more than that," Wingate said, with something like a sneer. "Everybody secretly thinks he or she looks like some movie star. Someone who does movie stars is therefore the right person to do *me*."

"Okay, wise guy," she challenged him. "Who do you look like?"

"I can formulate the law because I am outside it. In order to use Wingate's Law you have to be a Wingate."

Skipwith: "Have you ever used this codicil of Wingate's Law?"

"Do I look like Clark Gable?"

"Even less than I do."

"Yet you asked me, once, how I did so well with women in that Freak Records affair?"

"Yes."

"Well, part of the program was to say each woman looked like some particular actress. She was bound to be flattered if I chose a halfway presentable one—for fatsos, call on Mae West. But if I happened to hit the precise one she already thought of as her double, I instantly became the world's most perceptive man in her eyes. I was bound to her. Hadn't I *recognized* her?"

"Chauvinist pigs should not talk about fatsos," Marcia said heatedly. "And your 'law' is just a slander. I'm sure lots of people never thought of themselves as resembling movie stars."

"Including you?"

"Including me."

"Not even Julie Christie?"

"Of course not," she replied; but she also blushed.

Back in the apartment, the men changed clothes while Marcia studied a map of New Orleans in the front room. "I think I'll go for a stroll in the Quarter while you're gone."

Skipwith asked Wingate if that would be safe. "Sure. The Quarter's the safest place in the city; it's a playground with a lot of kids and indulgent cop-parents. Take that back. There is one safer spot—Audubon Place. Some typical millionaires bought their own street and created their own police force. Slatkin lived there till he fixed up his plantation. Now his son has the Audubon Place house."

After telling Marcia to be careful, Skipwith began to put on his dinner jacket. "Leave it off," Wingate warned. "We have a couple of blocks to swelter through before we get to the boat." At the Jackson Square landing, the rented paddlewheel *Huck Finn* had been waiting since 6:30. The two reached it just before the gangplank was raised. "Let's get into the air-conditioned lounge," Wingate said, shrugging on his jacket.

"Wait," Skipwith protested. He had not seen the Quarter's river front yet. The tropical sun was coming down through feather-siftings of cloud. The cathedral glowed in fire-settlings toward the grey ash of evening. "I don't get it," Skipwith said after watching the spectacle in silence. "We're on the Mississippi, right?"

"Right."

"And New Orleans is on the eastern bank of the Mississippi, right?"

"Right."

"Then the sun is setting in the east."

"Par for the New Orleans course. You know how you spin the blinded person who's 'it' in blindman's bluff?"

"Yeah."

"That's what the Mississippi does to people who get in its coils here."

"That's an explanation?"

"Who can explain?"

Wingate wanted to get inside, where the others were. Skipwith, seeing this, said, "Go on. I want to see the river bank after we cast off." They were shouting now. A jazz band had struck up as the lines were cast off. The players sweated out their music on the foredeck. Wingate said, "At least let me see if Slatkin's on the boat," and slipped off. A man in a white jacket came out to Skipwith and offered him a choice from his tray.

"Sazerac or gin fizz?"

Skipwith took the sazerac, that drink first literally made from poison; it still had a touch of Louisiana rot to its taste. Wingate was back now, barely audible over the jazz band. "No, he's waiting at the house. Come in and see Jack."

"No," Skipwith shouted into the trumpet-torn wind.

"That's the price we pay for Louis Armstrong, the perpetual tin flatulence—all these mini-Hirts farting sounds at you wherever you turn." Just then the cornetist put in a mute, for velvety crepitations. "Look at the cargo ship." Skipwith saw what he was pointing at—a hammer and sickle on the control tower. "See? Leander Perez was right. Let the niggers up, and soon there will be commies in Louisiana."

The boat had already made two sharp turns around the bending river, and Skipwith could see the Marriott Hotel over intervening land. "I still have no sense of direction."

Wingate tried to explain. "Imagine a golf club, a wood. The shaft points north. The Mississippi trickles in from the left (if you look at the golfer head-on), dips down and follows the head of the club around its surface—then the Quarter is on the *face* of the club. The Mississippi then curls off, after taking this tuck in its course. They call it the Crescent City. They should call it the Brassie."

Skipwith's sweat was cooling in the breeze caused by the boat's progress. Others began to filter out on deck. Skipwith's eyes were glued on the changing shoreline. They went past dim shipyards shoveling in Turnerian coal by night.

"They should call this Eddy's Alley."

"Why?"

"For all the money Hébert has shoveled into it as chairman of the Armed Services Committee."

"Slatkin should have picked us up later, when the night cooled this shore."

"Couldn't. River won't be high enough to reach his wharf by an hour from now. For the same reason, we have to leave around midnight."

Skipwith let himself be led inside by Wingate, and they helloed and shook hands through the crowd toward Jack Lewis.

"Hi, Jack. I hear you've been conscripted to lie about Wingate, same as me."

"Yes. I don't know why my word should matter on this. My students don't give it much weight in the area I *do* know about."

Wingate was quick to reassure: "Slatkin knows your work on Otway's *Venice Preserved*. He figures anyone who knows that story must be up on plots and conspiracies."

"Not as much as you obviously are."

"Good! Just tell him that!"

For the rest of the trip, Skipwith was treated like visiting royalty; old club members came round to tell him how glad they were he had joined them again. Glad? They sounded more relieved. Skipwith was not glad to see how hard trust came to him now.

It was not long before Wingate drew him back outside. "We're almost there."

The boat was swooping through muck near the levee. Trees loomed as a denser fuzz on velvety air; old trees had Spanish moss hanging like ear-hair from their addled heads. The paddlewheel was lifting mud now. The captain swung it in till its bow steadied with a slurp. The gangplank just reached the levee. Glasses still in their hands, the party clinked across the gangplank, crewmen steadying the more timorous, and went through the mothy dark toward Slatkin's brightly lit columns. The house was square on the French plan, arcade dark beneath and huge roofed gallery around the second (main) floor. Up on the brilliant gallery, a chill hit them through the triple-hung window door, chill and darkness. But as they entered, it became a darkness visible, a play of light on and through glass and mirrors and something that looked like Lucite. The architect had scooped out the entire three-story area, enclosed it in an air-conditioned box, and hung various levels of floors, steps, balconies, rooms.

Everyone looked first to the square in the center of this box, the Addison collection. Slatkin had brought sample items to various meetings; but most members were seeing the entire treasure for the first time. The walkway to the box was walled with glass, and men wavered through it like fish prismed in their tanks.

This liquid interior was edged and sparkling, unlike the spongy river air outside. Glass pipes carried ice water to various taps; a sculptor had shaped their zig-zag across one entire wall. Wingate nudged Skipwith aside, and said: "He has his own water supply—he thinks the parish system may have fluoride."

"Surely Louisiana does not fluoridate its water."

"Of course not. But Slatkin thinks the communists may inject fluoride secretly. Luckily, he thinks all conspirators as rich as he is."

"What are you getting yourself into?"

"He's no loonier than half the benefactors of Ivy League colleges. If we swore off kook money, we'd have to close most of our private institutions."

"That's the best argument I've heard for tax-run schools and the federal bureaucracy."

"You'd rather take your money from the workingman than from the addled rich?"

Skipwith yielded with a grimace. "And that?" he said, pointing to a glassy transpicuous pole.

"Fire pole for the frisky." The architect had connected his various levels with ramps, stairs, a slide, and this fireman's pole.

Slatkin came up as the two men stared at the pole. "Damn thing costs me as much in accident insurance as the whole rest of the house." Slatkin, straight as the pole and lean as a fireman, was in his sixties. He had made his money thirty years ago from chemicals. The panels and railings that bent and hosed light were not really Lucite but a synthetic his firm had developed. By making the house a showplace for all its uses, and bringing major clients to the house on weekends, he had written off half its expense as a business deduction. Even his luxuries made him money. With his crinkly eyes and David Niven mustache, he looked more a playboy than the driving businessman, but he had no hobbies except Addison; had never held a golf club; never played a card game.

Slatkin had Lewis in tow, and he boomed out, nonconspiratorially, "Here are our plotters all assembled—just don't plot against me." He laughed, but did not mean it to be funny. He shook hands with Wingate and Skipwith, hugging shoulders with his left hand at the same time—both his hug and handshake were hard. Business associates of Slatkin called this act of his "Squeezin' the shit out." If you doubted you were up against a tough customer, he disabused you with rough kindness from the outset. His whole manner said, "I'm a good man to have on your side."

He went to the point, with no other amenities: "You know what I want from you, and why?" Skipwith and Lewis nodded.

"A lot could ride on this. Perhaps the fate of the Republic." The two looked cold-feet looks at each other; but how to pull out now?

"You know I don't give a shit for all those academic letters after a man's name. I've got a bunch of 'em myself—honorary degrees from all those schools I donate to. I need a man who knows how to make decisions, out of experience and knowledge. I know Ben's got the experience. As men of knowledge yourselves, would you swear to his honest study of history where conspiracies are concerned?"

"Swear is a big word," Lewis hedged.

"Damn right it is. I'm not asking for any little piss-ant recommendation that he get some department's tenure. If Ben is good enough, he'll get the scholars working for him; but he has to be a judge of their work. And that's why I have to get your judgment on him."

Through this bullying performance, Skipwith kept thinking how typical it was of Wingate to involve him this way—never again, he was swearing as Slatkin looked a demand at him, and he spoke: "Everything I say must be taken in an Addisonian sense."

"The very thing I want." Slatkin obviously had not read his Dickens along with his Addison.

"I have known Ben longer than anyone here, and I recommended him for the club precisely because his knowledge of the Tudor-Stuart police state and religious underground give him a unique background for eighteenth-century studies. I gave my warrant for that, and of course I stand by it."

"Couldn't say fairer! Jack?"

"I've known Ben for a shorter time than Gregory, but everything I know confirms what Gregory says. You must remember, I seconded Ben's nomination for At Button's." He said it realizing how much Slatkin prized his own membership in this club, where he was the only businessman now that

Skipwith had given up executive office. What Lewis could *not* realize was that Slatkin, working on the Groucho Marx principle, had a lingering doubt about Wingate only *because* he was as clearly an outsider at Button's as was Slatkin himself. Lewis inadvertently resolved that doubt while feeling new doubts himself about this whole proceeding. Addison had somehow gone warrant for Wingate. The party could begin.

"This calls for champagne," Slatkin cried, and led the three around a curled wall into his study. Dom Perignon stood in a little wine box by his desk, always kept at forty-four degrees Fahrenheit.

The meeting went well. A paper on Addison's patrons paid indirect compliment to Slatkin for his generosity. The boyish stuffiness that had drawn Skipwith to the club became almost prankish in these eccentric surroundings. Three or four professors claimed they would slide down the glass firepole before they left, and two actually did it. When they heard the steamboat hoot from the landing, Wingate grabbed two bottles of champagne, watched Edward Bromberg ride majestically down the pole, and the heated company paddled through gooey air, so many aging Huck Finns, to board the *Huck Finn*.

Skipwith walked alone, testing old memories as one does an aching tooth. "Forget it," Wingate said, coming up beside him and handing him a bottle of champagne. On the boat, Lewis came over to them and said, "I'm afraid of that old bird. Is it true the pipe-sculpture is there to be sure his water is unfluoridated?" Wingate hesitated, but Skipwith nodded yes.

Then Wingate swept his hand, spilling champagne. "What's a little silliness in a man like that? He's like a cripple who becomes an athlete. To overcome his handicap increases his power and significance."

"Bullshit," Skipwith muttered. "You told us we were there to vouch for your knowledge of past history. He asked us to endorse your good judgment, which is like praising Attila's good manners. How typical of you."

"Typical of me? I only wanted your words on my book learning. It's typical of *him* to make everyone he deals with overcommit himself."

"That's true," Skipwith said with a smile. "You may have met your match, Wingate." He relaxed somewhat; and asked Lewis how he was enjoying his stay in New Orleans, how long he would be there.

"My wife and I are spending three days; it is our first visit."

Wingate invited Lewis and his wife over for a nightcap. "My wife will be asleep; but I can join you for a moment if you are near the Monteleone Hotel."

"Near enough."

iv

Shortly after the two men left Wingate's apartment, Marcia tried on her streetwalking jeans; realized they would be too hot; changed into shorts. She was anxious to get out, and her first look up and down the street told her why. The sun had disappeared in a mascara-smear; but the raffish houses glowed still, their balcony skirts askew. Despite an almost perceptible air of bustle in the Quarter—how *do* they do it in the heat? she asked herself—Dumaine Street was deserted except for a crewcut man in the next block sifting through garbage. She turned toward Bourbon Street, or so she thought. But at Chartres (oh, that's what Wingate called "Charters") could see market buildings along the river. Even her brief work on the map told her this was wrong, and she turned what she took to be upriver. Jackson Square drew her, she liked the open clutter of it. But then a policeman crooked his finger for her to come over. New York habits made her bristle; "What is it, *officer?*" she asked, sinking her voice and (she hoped) him on the last word.

"These folks can't find a match. I thought you might help them." An old couple seated on a bench had been chatting with him; the man still fumbled with his pipe and pouch. Marcia laughed with relief, said she had no match, but went over and bummed one from an artist who was smoking and sketching with equal fury—so easily does New Orleans recruit one.

In the arcade of the Cabildo, three raggedy young musicians wrestled with Vivaldi's Trio in D-flat. Only the girl with the flute was poised, but they were all good. When they passed the hat afterward, Marcia tried to talk with the flautist; but she was too busy sorting music sheets. The boy on cello said, "Don't interfere with the impresario. She drives us more here than at the conservatory."

"What conservatory?"

"Peabody. Do you know it?"

"No."

"It's in Baltimore—another port city. Makes me feel at home here."

"I know some port cities, but they just make this look more foreign to me."

"Why?"

Marcia stepped back to look at the Cabildo. "This is an odd fortress. The church overpowers it. New Orleans is the least defended old-world port I've ever seen."

"Oh, New Orleans was always more easily bought than conquered. Its best buildings have always been its banks." He gestured up: "A fort with frilly cast-iron railings—doesn't look quite serious, does it?"

She agreed. "But I remember studying a battle of New Orleans in school."

"That was fought downriver, and was a land battle. They tried to fortify the river front, but the Mississippi wouldn't put up with it. It nibbles forts away. Even this garrison, far from the shore, was always more for entertaining than for training."

"I come from New York," Marcia told him, "and I find it hard to think of this as a world port."

"It is, though, third largest in the world. Even New York is only second. But there can't be any clustering of piers. The shore's too mushy, for one thing. And the river's too narrow to poke things out into it. Boats have to park parallel to the shore, not 'nose in.' The port just straggles along for miles downriver."

They had strolled over to the front of the cathedral, while the cellist smoked his between-trios cigarette. Marcia noticed idly the crewcut man standing back in the arcade of the Presbytere. Surely there was no garbage for the picking there? The flautist was calling her conservatory bums back to work; Marcia asked, "Bourbon that way?" He nodded and she turned. But, remembering that she had put nothing in the hat, she turned back suddenly, rounded the corner, and almost bumped into Crewcut. "Pardon me," she said, but he did not even look up. After dropping her dollar in the hat as quicky as she could, she rushed back into St. Peter Street—and saw no Crewcut. She remembered what Wingate had said about the safety of the Quarter, shrugged her shoulders, and went on. She passed black women and their daughters playing bingo in a churchyard.

Bourbon Street released jets of cool air and hot music from open doors. At one point she thought a music hall had come out to the middle of the street and begun to follow her; then she realized it was just a young man with his transistor radio on at full volume. Even the balconies loosed stereo jazz in the air, one stridency canceling others, making a pleasant jumble—as with the garishness in general.

She thought: More Coney Island, this, than Lexington Avenue. A talker, swinging open a door for glimpses of a nude dancer, droned: "Family entertainment here. Lessons in anatomy. Approved by the Sorbonne."

"Does that really draw them in?" she asked the young man.

"Naw. But it keeps me awake. You looking for a job?" He eyed her legs.

"Hardly."

"Oh, we're not so bad here. We don't recycle the beer, we just recycle bums in the audience." He lifted his voice: "Come to Bums' Paradise."

"Can your boss hear you?"

"She's up north—too smart to stay in this heat." Marcia went in. A girl in G-string and bikini top seated her. The dancers obviously waited when not on stage. "Could I talk to you during your break?"

"We're not the lesbies, honey; that's two bars down," she gestured.

"I'm not a lesbian. I'm a sociologist."

"I never heard of that one, but I'm sure we've got a place for it if you just keep asking."

Marcia had never seen her girls in New York as naked as this, but she knew they did not have suntans with bikini marks. The dancers looked more like beach bums at a disco than the spangled and stockinged whores of Marcia's experience. The place was sleazy, but its nakedness was healthy and almost antiseptic. Marcia put away her notebook.

Later peeks into this or that dance place showed the same crop of slim shakers—one was doing a grind while standing on her head. There was no stripping or tease. Just naked on, shake-shake, and naked off. Only one joint kept its door resolutely closed, so she resolutely pushed in. It was the "Boys and Girls Together" place—a chubby girl flopping around, making mouth snatches at the athletic boy's jockstrap. Only boys waited on table, and they were all prettier than the one girl chunking away onstage. Noticing that she was the only other woman in the place, Marcia left even before her two-dollar thimble of beer arrived.

Her relief as she came out was checked when she saw Crewcut turn to peek into a girly show across the street. She suddenly lost her taste for Bourbon Street, and headed down Toulouse for Chartres. Near Jackson Square, she stopped to look in a shop window, and glanced to her right—the street was clear one moment, crowded the next, in the Quarter's inexplicable way; but she saw no Crewcut. When she heard a chaconne coming from the trio, she laughed at her fears and stood to listen. The cello player came over at the break and thanked her for the dollar she had put in the hat. He lit his cigarette in front of the cathedral, and chatted. "Like Bourbon Street?"

"Love it."

"Why?"

"It's exciting without being wicked."

"Don't be too sure of that." He turned to blow smoke and said quietly, "Is that man following you?" Crewcut was back at the Presbytere—he must have circled ahead of her, guessing her route.

"He—he might be."

"Good, then he's not stalking *me*. Are you going far?"

"Just a block or two."

"Wait one more piece, and I'll walk you there."

"Thank you."

They saw no more of Crewcut. She had no reason to trust this stranger more than that other one. But she did. He gave his name: Keith. She did not ask for a last one, for fear of sounding suspicious. After he took her to the apartment and up the stairs, she asked, halfheartedly, "Come in?"

"Monica would kill me if I'm not back. The only duet we have, Betty does in spurts and stops, throwing Monica's time off. Come by and hear us again."

"I will." Now she was a little afraid to be left alone. She turned on a dull public network show, and pretended she was in New York where it was made.

At one o'clock she was almost asleep when Skipwith and

Wingate came in with a stranger, introducing him as Jack Lewis. "Have a good tour of the Quarter?" Wingate asked her.

"Yes. But I thought you said it was safe."

"Wasn't it?"

"I don't know. I think I was followed."

"From where?"

"Here."

"And all the way back?"

"I can't be sure, but I think so."

"What did he look like?"

"Thirty or so, crewcut, slim; pants like a sailor's, kind of floppy; and a T-shirt." Wingate went out while Skipwith kept questioning her—where did she see him, how often, how close? Wingate was soon back. "No one there. Did anyone else see him?"

"A street musician in Jackson Square."

"Let's go."

"Keith's probably gone."

"We'll see."

Lewis asked, shyly, "May I come too? Nothing like a little adventure to round off a trip to New Orleans."

"Sure. We still owe you a drink."

The trio of musicians had gone off by the time they reached the Square, but Marcia saw Keith drinking milk in the Pontalba Bar's open arcade. He confirmed Marcia's description for Wingate; and said he had kept an eye out for Crewcut after taking her to the apartment, but had not seen him.

"Let's have that drink," Wingate said. Marcia invited Keith along. Skipwith wondered why he did not think that a good idea.

They trailed down the center of the street, so water would not hit them from the balconies. Denizens were out at night watering tropical gardens on the iron railings. They went past Bourbon Street, and Wingate pointed. "See that pink and white place? Clay Shaw's home. When he died, Tennessee Williams moved in." They wound back to Bourbon, more downriver, and into a private club Wingate behonged to. The five of them went out onto a balcony and ordered sazeracs all around.

"Is that a pimp?" Marcia asked, still trying to adjust new experience to old research. "He has the right kind of hat." But as he came nearer their balcony, she saw he was wearing a mesh shirt with the nipples sticking through, skintight jeans, and no shoes. "Not pimp style, I'm afraid."

Wingate told her: "Pimps here own real estate, not a string of girls. Girls go with the houses and bars. Our pimps only dress up as part of the Krewes at Mardi Gras time."

Keith, whose last name was Farrell, chimed in: "The girls in Jackson Square are free-lance. They have to try hard to get a cop's attention, and then he just tells anyone dumb enough to get caught in Jackson Square she—or he—has chosen the wrong profession."

"How unorganized," Marcia said, yearning to go back to her rules and timetables.

"Therefore civilized," Keith argued.

Wingate laughed. "Huck Finn, meet Margaret Mead. She has something to learn from you."

Two burly men, dressed twinsy-style in identical tight pants and tanktops, swaggered along, linked by their pinkies.

"That reminds me," Skipwith said. "Does Clay Shaw figure in the conspiracy?" Marcia noticed that he referred to "the conspiracy" now, as to a definite thing.

"No, but some of his associates do."

"You mean the Jolly Green Giant was onto something after all?"

"Garrison? He was on it like an elephant on bird tracks. If I never crack this case, it will be because of Jim Garrison. Though I have to admit he opened new possibilities for me."

"How?"

"Even while he was district attorney, he drew on private money to investigate the assassination. Then he made the mistake of bringing in leftie freaks like Mark Lane and Mort Sahl and Dick Gregory. That scared away good Louisiana money, which wanted Oswald to be a commie. My first approach to Slatkin was patriotic, in the narrow Louisiana sense. Did he want outside money to come in and frame good conservative New Orleanians?"

"Just what have you got?" It was Lewis, still sounding skeptical.

"I'll show you tomorrow."

"Not me. My wife will think I deserted her if we don't tour the Quarter tomorrow."

v

The next day, Wingate drove Skipwith and Marcia up River Road to Elba, Slatkin's plantation. "Jefferson bought this place from Napoleon, but you see fifty things commemorating Napoleon for every one that recalls Jefferson."

"There's Jefferson County."

"Yeah. But most people around here think of Jefferson Davis when you say Jefferson. It's good Thomas Jefferson never saw what he was buying."

"Why?"

"He hated cities, even a clean Quaker place like Philadelphia. What would he have made of New Orleans, rank with all of Europe's sins and superstitions? You know the Spanish tried to set up a court of the Inquisition in New Orleans?"

"So Jim Garrison has a long pedigree."

At Elba, they found that Slatkin was in town. Wingate, familiar to the staff, showed Marcia through the manor house, then took the two to his "garçonnière" where files and films were kept, guarded by Avory Nelson. "Avory worked for the *Dallas Morning News* along with Hugh Aynesworth. But he was not so gullible as Aynesworth. He brought his own good files into the project when I reached him."

A light outside the door told them Nelson was developing film, so they knocked and waited. "We can't trust these films to a commercial developer."

Nelson finally opened the door, not happy that others were going to be admitted with Wingate. "Don't worry. They helped us with Slatkin."

"Do they know the dangers involved?"

"No. Because they'll run no dangers. Unless Marcia becomes a research assistant."

"What are the dangers in that?" Skipwith asked warily.

"None for mere assistants. And probably none for directors. Nelson flatters himself that others put as high a value on his life, for the taking, as he puts on it for the keeping."

Wingate was fiddling with movie projectors. "Do you remember that Oswald worked, here in New Orleans, for a Luzianne coffee distributor?"

"No."

"Well, he did. And he had a black friend at the plant he often mentioned to Marina. But no one ever found him, and most people say Oswald made him up. We know better, don't we, Avory?" Avory grunted, and flicked off the lights.

Two projectors whirred together. The left one showed an image of a young black strapped to a lie detector. The one on the right showed the needles of the polygraph machine, darting and stabbing like the legs of a praying mantis. The black was caught in mid-sentence: "—found I was a homosexual, and broke off our friendship. Lee couldn't even stand to hear dirty jokes around the shop. So I looked one day in his lunchbox to see if I could embarrass him. I found a list of telephone numbers, and put it in my pocket . . ."

Wingate turned off the projectors. "That's all you should hear for now. Can you read a polygraph?"

"No," they chorused.

"If you could, you would see he passed with flying colors. The same is true of all that follows. He's our key to the whole case."

"Is he here?"

"No, we've got him in hiding. My first big sum from Slatkin was to hire two full-time guards for him and establish a place where no one else can reach him."

"Why all the precautions?"

"Someone is onto us, maybe the government. We found a tap on our phone. We sweep this place for bugs every day. That must be why you were followed, Marcia. They wondered why you were in my apartment. Would you feel safer at a hotel?"

"No," she said, though Skipwith was looking dubious. "We're only staying one more night."

As he drove back into New Orleans, Wingate took them by Oswald's house on Magazine Street, and Reily's coffee plant. "His contacts were all made at the plant, none at his home. We are going to track down every employee of Reily's once our staff is expanded." Wingate dropped them off at his apartment. "I'll be back at eight. You should eat at Le Ruth's your last night in New Orleans. We'll drive across the river."

Skipwith wanted to go watch the sun set behind the cathedral again, but Marcia was tired and took a nap. He strolled over and bought a double sazerac at the Pontalba Bar. One of the things he liked best about the city was the way people could take drinks out as they strolled or sat. It made all of New Orleans an outdoor cafe.

The sun ripened, split, spread a glory of rot around the cathedral—the very sazerac of churches. He felt life stirring in him, strong after all, despite his three years of hibernation. How silly it had been to oppose Wingate. Wingate was tricky, but . . .

Wingate was running toward him, out of the alley by the

cathedral. He looked right and left, at those walking in the square. Skipwith was up, now, waving to him from his bench.

"They've kidnapped Marcia," he said and handed Skipwith a note, too breathless to say more. It read: "End your investigation if you want to see her again."

"Who's behind this?"

"I might know."

"Get the police."

"No."

"Why not?"

"The local police could be cooperating with the kidnappers."

"Then the FBI."

"You only get to them through the police."

"We have to do something."

"I will."

"Good. You do what you can. I'm calling the police."

Wingate gripped his arm, dragged him: "Come to the apartment and calm down. I tell you, I think I know who's behind this. Those who were tapping Garrison's money sources. They don't want Slatkin interfering. He will dry up all other money. No businessmen will cross him."

"So what does Marcia have to do with this?"

"I think they'll want a straight swap. Marcia for that film I showed you." They went up the stairs and into the apartment. Skipwith ran around checking rooms, which made no sense.

"What is the point of getting your film?"

"They'll use it to shut me up. It's a fake."

"A *what*?"

"The man's an actor. The polygraph was rigged. I never intended to use it as part of the real investigation. I did it to shake some people loose around here, to turn up real leads. I pretended I had a witness, to make them think the truth was bound to come out anyway, they might as well talk. But if the other side gets hold of the film, they'll claim I meant to go public with it unless I withdraw."

"So the black man is not really in custody?"

"Like hell he isn't. They'd just as soon get him as the film. All they have to do is produce one or the other to undo me."

"Well, get goddam un*done* then. Get Marcia back."

"It's not that simple. These people have Mafia ties. The Jolly Green Giant loved to investigate everybody but the Mafia, you remember. If Marcia can identify her abductors, she's likely to suffer an accident no matter what we do."

"What do you propose, then?"

"I can get to two of their people, but I'll need help. Some private detectives I know could pull it off—two here, two in New York. We'll also need some bribe money."

"Slatkin's got plenty."

"This money must never be traced to Slatkin. You know how the IRS paws over foundation finances."

"Damn the foundation. Forget it."

"You don't want Slatkin prowling around, do you, nutty as he is? We can't use him. Do you know where to get money fast?"

"How much?"

"Oh, twelve thou for investigators, maybe thirty for bribes. Say fifty thou to be safe."

"I'll call Ralston. You know him?"

"Sure. Another foundation man." Skipwith rang New York, but Ralston was out. He left a message, calling the matter urgent. "What now?"

"I'll call my New York men, to get them moving. Then I'll pick up the local talent."

"Can't you call them?"

"They'll be on the move; I'll have to track them."

"I'm coming with you."

"You can't. You have to take Ralston's call and get the money here by morning."

"I hate to be stranded here. How will I get in touch with you?"

"You won't. Call Jack Lewis over. He wanted some adventure."

Skipwith watched, with panic, as Wingate took off his coat, fitted a shoulder holster, took a gun from behind a panel in his wall. "I'll get you one of these."

"No you won't. It's not happening again."

"What's not?" Wingate eyed him appraisingly. "Get hold of yourself. Have a brandy." And he left.

Skipwith called Lewis at the Monteleone, but got no answer. He left word to call. He felt chained, isolated from the world, unable to reach out. Everyone else was moving, while he sat. He took the telephone over to the balcony, dragging his chain, and opened the door. A girl bicycled down the street, her baby on her back like a papoose.

"Help!" he called, feeling genuine fear in a fake situation. "Here's five dollars. Would you peddle by the Cabildo and tell a cellist named Keith playing there that Marcia needs him this very minute?"

She frowned, wondering what game this was; but took the five dollars that came spinning down to her, folded like a sailing maple seedlet. "If you're nuts, thanks anyway. I'll look for Keith if you'll tell me you're not Marcia."

"Of course I'm not."

In less than ten minutes, Keith buzzed the patio door and clattered up the stairs. "I'm sorry, but the girl on the bicycle waited until we finished a sonata movement. What's happened?" Skipwith told him.

"What can we do?"

"I have no idea. But I had to have someone to talk it over with."

The phone rang. Ralston. "Look, Samuel, I know this sounds

crazy, but Marcia is in trouble and we may need money to get her out."

"Is it that Wingate fellow?"

"In a way."

"He seems to carry trouble with him. How much?"

"Fifty thousand to be safe. We'll pay you back. Can you wire it?"

"I can wire it. I'll also fly it down in one of the company jets. Make a reservation for me at the Marriott, ask for my regular room. I'll call you when I get in." He hung up before Skipwith could say anything.

Neither Skipwith nor Farrell slept that night, but the phone did not ring again. It was nine o'clock when Ralston called from the Marriott. "Shall I come there or you here?"

"You better come here. We have to watch this phone."

"We? Who's there?"

"A local friend."

"Leave him at the phone. I think we'll need the hotel's facilities."

He got a cab on Chartres; saw it poke and pause through tourists; got out, and ran to the Marriott. When he finished, Ralston went to the phone and called the airport. "I brought some security people from the corporation. They may be useful. I'll put them in the room next door."

Shelly came in while Ralston was on the phone. Shook hands. Said, "You like?" He had bought a T-shirt with a Mississippi steamboat on it, and—lettered underneath—"The Delta Queen." Ralston gave him an irritated glance, and said one word as he hung up: "Off." Shelly took off his shirt and sat down. Ralston asked Skipwith for more on the actor in Wingate's film. Before long Shelly got up, went to the bedroom, came back out in a different shirt, and left without a word.

The phone rang. It was Farrell asking for Skipwith. "Wingate just called and asked if we had the money. I said yes, and that Ralston had come too."

"Where is Wingate?"

"He wouldn't say."

"Did he say anything?"

"When I told him Ralston had come, he said something about speeding up 'the movement by Main.' Is there a Main Street here?"

"I don't know. I suppose there's one in every city." Ralston asked for the phone and told Farrell, "I'm sending a man over to be your messenger if you need one. Call us here if anything turns up."

Lewis tried for Skipwith at Wingate's apartment, and was given the Marriott number. Skipwith told him: "I can't tell you what's happening on the phone. We're trying to keep this line clear. Come over and we'll fill you in."

Three of Ralston's security men had arrived now and he ordered one over to Wingate's apartment. Then he ordered lunch for six. They were eating when Lewis arrived. Skipwith told him all they knew. There was nothing to do but wait. Skipwith kept wanting to try Wingate's phone. But Ralston snapped at him to sit down and trust Farrell. The habit of command came easily when Ralston was not just auditioning people for grants.

At two, Shelly came in with a young black. "I think I know where Wingate's actor is being held—Bayou Acadiane."

"What?"

"I found the local actors' hangout, The Shackled Pirate. Joseph here got a message from his lover, sent through a trapper's daughter, saying he was being held against his will. Joseph followed the girl back into the bayou, but the boat with the man who gave her the message was gone."

Ralston asked Joseph: "What kind of boat was it?"

"I never saw it. The girl said a houseboat."

"Color?"

"Green and white."

Ralston thought a minute, then dialed. "Farrell, do you know where to rent a fishing boat?"

"Sure."

"Leave my man on the phone. Go rent us a fast boat and a guide—make sure the guide knows Bayou Acadiane. Call me when you have it."

Lewis drew Skipwith aside: "There may be nothing to this, I've been thinking of Wingate's comment, what Farrell heard as 'by Main Street.' Wingate was particularly interested in the Bye and the Main Plots."

"What were they?"

"I don't remember. I was always intrigued by the spelling of the By, for Side, Plot as B-Y-E. But it has been years since I looked at the matter; Wingate's references were always too vague for me to know what he meant by them."

"Tell Ralston." They had all begun to rely on this little operation's commander. Ralston heard Lewis out, then said, "Your conspiracy lady in the reading room would know about this, wouldn't she?" Skipwith nodded. "Call her."

"I don't know her last name."

Ralston called the reading room and asked for the guard on duty. It was not Ed Jones. Ralston described the conspiracy lady, but the guard could find no one like that in the room. "The Babe?" Ralston asked Skipwith, who nodded. He described Sybil into the phone. The guard knew her all right. He put her on the line. Ralston asked if the conspiracy lady was around.

"No. Why?"

"Do you know her last name?"

"No."

"Could you find her?"

"I can try. What's the matter?"

"Marcia's in trouble. Have the conspiracy lady call us as soon as you find her."

Ralston was pacing up and down now. "We're accomplishing

nothing here. Lewis, take a cab to Tulane and see what you can find on those plots in the library. Skipwith, you take the public library. Call if you get anything. There will be someone on this phone all the time."

Within an hour both Lewis and Skipwith had returned, each grumbling about the inadequate library they had to deal with. "How does anyone live in a town without a decent library?"

Ralston said, "Don't worry. Sybil found a reader who knew the conspiracy lady and she phoned. I had a stenographer up to take her message. What do you make of it?"

Skipwith read the first copy and Lewis the carbon. "It doesn't help much, does it?"

"Maybe not. I told the conspiracy lady—whose name is Schreiber—I'd pay her to sit by the phone if we get any questions for her. Sybil said she was coming down, so I got a company jet for her."

"Christ, we're emptying out New York and it doesn't get us anywhere. Why is Sybil coming?"

"Because she's Marcia's friend."

"Funny way she showed it—lying to her."

Ralston looked genuinely puzzled. Then said, as if to himself, "All friends have funny ways of showing it."

Then he smiled, and Skipwith resented that. "What could be funny at a time like this?"

"I've never seen you so angry—or alive."

"I've never seen you such a prick before . . ." He threw a hand up as if trying to catch the word, bring it back. "I'm . . . Pay no attention to me."

Ralston put his hand on his shoulder. "Take it easy. We'll find her."

"Where the hell is Wingate?"

"I don't know. But Farrell called to say he has a boat. Who will search the bayou?" No one answered Ralston's question; so he answered it himself. "Keith, Shelly, Joseph, and one security man will go. I'll rent a backup boat, in radio contact with the first, in case they need help. The security man is armed, but he's not to use his gun unless attacked. If force is needed, we'll call in the police.

"Skipwith, you go to the airport and pick up Sybil. She'll want to be filled in on what happened to Marcia. Lewis, call the Schreiber lady and see if you can't get more clues from her." Skipwith suspected Ralston was enjoying his own unaccustomed decisiveness. He ignored the order to get to the airport, and asked: "Why aren't we looking for Wingate?"

"Where should we look?"

"Maybe his journalist partner at Elba knows where he might be."

"Good idea. Do you know how to reach Elba?"

"Yes. It's just out River Road."

"Rent a car and go there. You go right past the airport. You can pick up Sybil." It was now just Ralston's way to get his way. Skipwith hoped he was as successful with Marcia's kidnappers as he was proving with him.

He had to ask at the airport for the place where private jets come in. Since Sybil had no definite landing time, he studied the map while he waited for her—a half-hour. He only called Ralston twice in that time.

Sybil had no luggage. She had obviously gone straight from the library to the plane. "Where's Marcia?"

"Still missing. That's what we're trying to find out. I'll explain in the car." He showed her their destination on the map, and let her guide him. Between directions he recounted the events of the last two days.

"This Wingate sounds dangerous."

"Yeah. I hope more dangerous to their side than to ours."

"I think I better sleep with him."

"Why?"

"It takes off the mystery."

"Remind me not to sleep with you."

"I don't think you need reminding. Besides, I don't think I could face Marcia afterward."

"When did you become solicitous for Marcia—after all those lies you told her?"

"They weren't all lies. When did you get solicitous for her?"

"Who says I am?"

"This is the first time I've seen you when you weren't dim."

"Everybody's accusing me of vividness today. If putting a young woman in dangerous situations is the way to get color in my cheeks, I prefer to stay dim."

"Yes, Marcia told me about your fear of controlling others. Wouldn't you like to control her kidnappers now?"

"But that's the trouble. I affected her life, and the only way to repair that is to go on affecting others' lives. It's a vicious circle."

"Don't worry. It sounds like you're not controlling things. Ralston is. Why do you think he came himself, instead of just sending the money?"

"Friendship, I guess."

"Not a bad way of affecting other lives. I don't know if you got Marcia into this trouble. But you'll notice her friends are trying hard to get her out of it. Of course, there's Ralston's friendship for *you*—for your vulnerability, I'd say. You can trade too much on that you know. You passive people screw up people's lives just as much as the aggressive types. Your inaction forces other to act."

Skipwith was uncomfortable with this blunt conversation that sounded more like an accusation. It relieved him to see the addled trees of Elba with their straggle of moss. "We'll go direct to the garçonnière, and avoid Slatkin if we can. If he sees us, I'm just introducing you to Nelson as a possible research assistant."

They, knocked at the garçonnière, but got no answer. Skipwith tried the door, and it opened. Since there was only one room on each floor, a glance showed that the file room was empty. Skipwith went straight to the file on the black actor, pulled it out and looked rapidly through it. It was full of timetables, descriptions of meetings with Oswald, names to go with the phone numbers out of Oswald's lunch box—all the fake stuff, nothing on the actor himself or his act.

"What are you doing here?" When they turned, Nelson was on the stairway with a gun in his hand.

"What are *you* doing waving a gun at us?"

"Those files are not open to anyone but Wingate and me."

"Where is Wingate?"

"I don't know. I thought he was with you."

"Did you know Miss Roquist has been kidnapped?"

"Who's Miss Roquist?"

"The woman Wingate brought here with me. You don't seem surprised at her kidnapping."

"Should I be?"

"Have you ever heard of something called the Bye Plot or the Main Plot?"

"No."

"That's odd. Wingate mentioned them to a casual acquaintance like Jack Lewis, but never discussed them with you, his expert on conspiracy? I think we better go see Slatkin about this. I believe you're lying." He started toward the door. Nelson put one thumping bullet through the door. Skipwith drew back.

"You better stay here for a while." Nelson slid down the stairs and out the door, ramming its bolt home behind him. Skipwith ran to a window, but they had all been barred when the files were installed. Sybil ran upstairs and looked out another barred window toward the manor house. "That's odd. Nelson's going into the house, as if he were reporting to Slatkin."

"Maybe he wants to get his story to Slatkin first."

"Maybe Slatkin hired him to spy on your Wingate. You told me he is a suspicious businessman."

"No. Ben brought Nelson here from Dallas. Has he come out yet?"

"No."

"You keep watching the house while I look for something to pry these bars apart."

"I don't think you'll have much luck at that."

He could hear scraping on the floor above him. By the time he got upstairs, Sybil was standing on a table pushing at a trapdoor in the ceiling. "Come up here and help. I read about these garçonnières—they had entrances to the second floor entirely bypassing the first floor, so the young men of the house could keep their lady friends to themselves." Soon they were out on the roof, which showed traces of an old platform and outside stairs. But the wood had long ago rotted away, and the wall was a sheer drop of brick surface mottled with old stucco. A vine ran down the shaded side, but when Sybil put her foot into its tangle it shredded like cobweb. Skipwith pulled her back onto the roof. "Look," he said as he straightened up. Two men had come up over the levee and were heading for the house. "They must have a boat." The two shouted and waved their hands; but, though the men saw them, they made no response.

A few minutes later Slatkin came out of the house with Nelson and the two men. They were chatting amiably. Skipwith and Sybil shouted Slatkin's name, and he turned; recognized them; turned away, heading for the levee. "Be careful, Slatkin!" Skipwith shouted. "There's been one kidnapping already. You may be in danger." Slatkin just shook his head. Nelson fired a shot over the roof, making Skipwith duck down. He looked up to see Slatkin order Nelson to holster his gun— which Nelson did. They heard the boat's motor now, and saw it when it moved out from the levee—a large red motorboat, with only the four men in its open cockpit.

"If that tree were just a foot closer I could jump to it."

"The branches wouldn't hold you," she answered. "They would hold me."

"We'll have to make a rope. Let's go down and look for drapes, blankets, sheets. Anything to make a rope."

"Why don't we just look for a rope?" While he began tying blankets on the second floor, where Nelson slept, she found a rope that had tied one of the file cabinets shut in transit. Between the two of them they came up with twenty-five feet of soft and lumpy cable; but some of that had to be wasted in knottings around the trapdoor hinge, the sturdiest anchor they could find on the roof. Only fifteen feet actually hung down the wall. "That means about a twelve-foot drop."

"Watch your ankle, it's uneven ground," she told him while he tested the rope, pulling as hard as he could on the hinge; but it held. He dropped. Then she.

In the manor house, Skipwith brushed past a butler toward the phone. "Ralston? Any word on Marcia? We're at Elba. Nelson shot at us and locked us up, then took Slatkin away in a red motorboat, open cockpit. Maybe you should have the marine police pick them up."

"On what charge?"

"Possible kidnapping."

"Was Slatkin forced on the boat?"

"Not that we could tell."

"You stay there. I'll come upriver in our second fishing boat. If I see Slatkin, I'll try to talk to him. If not, I'll pick you up at the levee. Find out what you can from the hired help around there. Is there a Mrs. Slatkin?"

"No. He was a widower."

"I should see you within the hour. Report anything new to this phone. The stenographer is keeping a log."

They discovered nothing useful from the staff, except that

Slatkin's well-kept appointment book had nothing in it for this afternoon. His secretary was surprised when he left without saying where he would be. Skipwith was left with nothing to do but pace the gallery. Sybil interrupted him, partly because his prowling irritated her: "Tell me more about Wingate. How did you meet him?"

Briefly he told her about his days at Continent, and even a little about Harris's death in Wisconsin.

"What fascinated Wingate about the Bye and Main Plots?"

"Miss Schreiber says his theory is that the Bye Plot actually came first, and was bungled; but Sir Walter Raleigh drew participants of it into a bigger plot, for which he was agent provacateur."

"Why did he do that?"

"Again according to Wingate, to ingratiate himself with the new king, who thought of Raleigh as Elizabeth's man."

"Then maybe Wingate saw the Slatkin kidnapping as the Main Plot, for which Marcia's was just a trial run."

"If Wingate foresaw Slatkin's kidnapping, why wasn't he here to prevent it?"

"He may be stalking the kidnappers."

"Not very effectively. Slatkin's gone."

"Well, it's just a theory."

"Let's follow it through. How would kidnapping Marcia set up Slatkin?"

"Perhaps to throw guilt on Marcia's kidnappers."

"You mean, away from more obvious suspects?"

"Yes."

"But who *would* be suspected if Slatkin were kidnapped without Marcia's disappearance preceding his?"

"Business rivals? People after his money? Those involved in the conspiracy, if they thought Slatkin's money was about to expose them."

"*Or* rivals from past business wars. The list is endless. Why would it be to anyone's advantage to think Wingate's rival conspiratorialists were behind it, instead of more obvious people?"

"It could make Wingate seem more important."

"It also could get him into trouble with the law. He doesn't want word of his fake films to get around. The thing makes no sense."

She was sorry to give up her theory, but she had to agree with him.

A car had pulled into the drive and was tunneling through the old trees. Its door swung open even before it stopped, and Wingate was running toward the house. "Is Slatkin here?"

"No, he went off with Nelson." They came down from the gallery to meet him under the trees.

"I'm too late then. Nelson was a plant for the other side. I should have suspected it earlier. I tried to bargain for Marcia's return. I even promised them the films. But they said they'd stop me another way. They've either kidnapped Slatkin, or they're taking him to see my black actor. Either way the foundation scheme is finished. Now we've just got to get Marcia back."

"This time I *am* calling the police."

"You'll just screw things up."

"Too bad. Oh no, not again—I'm getting tired of having guns pulled on me today. You want to lock us up in the garçonnière? That didn't work with Nelson."

Ralston hailed them from the levee. They had not heard his boat arrive in the rush to talk with Wingate. Wingate looked toward Ralston over the lawn, backed toward his car, said, "Believe me, you'll endanger Marcia if you call the cops," and sped his car back out to the road, reversing his tires with a screech and leaping off toward New Orleans. Skipwith ran toward his rented car, but Sybil called, "Why chase him? We have to decide with Ralston about calling the police."

Ralston had Lewis with him. "We saw the red boat near New Orleans but it sped past us, making no response to our signals."

"Wingate just left here. He thinks Slatkin was kidnapped or is being taken to see the black actor. Have Keith and Shelly found that guy yet?"

"No. They know where the houseboat was docked three nights ago, and they're asking up and down the bayou for more recent sightings of it."

"Maybe it left the bayou for the inner waterway."

"I thought of that. It would be easy to spot there. I have a helicopter looking for it."

"You've got a goddamn army at work, and it's accomplishing nothing. It's cop time. Use the *state's* army."

"I think you're right. We'll go straight to them back in New Orleans. Coming with us on the boat?"

"One of us should return the rental car."

"Leave it. I'll tell them where it is."

On the boat, Skipwith tried Sybil's theory on Ralston, who liked it better than Skipwith had.

"You say it would not be to Wingate's advantage for his films to become public knowledge. Why would they have to?"

"How could they be kept a secret? Anything that happens to Slatkin is news."

"What if Slatkin continued to think the films real, and no one else heard of them?"

"Not with the nosy press aware that there had been a kidnapping."

"Maybe that could be hushed up as well—assuming there *was* a kidnapping."

"Too many assumptions for me." But Ralston had planted the seed of a terrible doubt in Skipwith's mind. He went off to see how it would grow. The hard spank of the boat as it skipped up and banged down on the water reminded him of his day on the Potomac with Lynn. The rush of air gave a sense of freedom, but the jolts were spaced out in chain lengths shackling him to his past, a liquid captivity. He thought of the weird passage in the Book of Job about God putting the water in bonds so it would not swallow the earth.

Sybil joined him. "My theory or a new one?"

"What?"

"What are you thinking about?"

"Something I have been refusing to see for three years."

"What?"

"You'll think me crazy if I tell you."

"Try me."

"I've half-known all along I'd have to destroy him. That's why I seceded from life. Every bit of life would have to be bought. I'd have to pay someday. Wingate would be the price."

"You're right. I think it, and you are it. Crazy."

"No. He's the price."

"He may be no gem. But don't you prefer him to Marcia's kidnappers?"

"There are no kidnappers. There's only Wingate."

"What do you mean? What of the men who took Slatkin away?"

"Wingate's men. There's never been anyone but Wingate. I know the way his mind works. He'll rescue Slatkin from his imagined rivals, making Slatkin value him more than ever. He'll end up with all of Slatkin's power and money at his disposal. He wants to be Raleigh behind the scenes, pulling all the strings—but this time making it work. I remember, now, his saying Raleigh's scheme was brilliant, but he bungled it."

"Can you stop Wingate?"

"I don't know. Maybe he and the world deserve each other."

"What does Marcia deserve?" He did not answer. "Shouldn't you tell Ralston what you think?" No answer. "I like my theory better."

"So do I."

"Still want to call the police in?"

"Let Ralston do it. I'm going to Wingate's apartment. He'll return there eventually. He may even have left some clue."

The radio in the boat's pulpit cabin was fading in and out. Ralston gestured for silence, and the others crowded in around him. "This is Shelly. We've found the boat. But there's no one in it. It's at a landing with six or seven cabins scattered near. No one has come out from them. Shall we search?"

"Where are you?"

"Near Delacroix."

"How far is that from New Orleans?" Ralston asked the captain of his boat, who shrugged: "Less than an hour."

"Shelly, stand off in your boat till we get there."

"If you're right," Sybil said to Skipwith, "Wingate may be going to check on his men with the black actor."

"*Or* on the ones holding Marcia. *Or* the ones who have Slatkin."

The radio buzzed again: "Shelly here. A red motorboat just landed, after coming close by us and looking us over. Luckily, we had started fishing to explain our presence."

"I think you caught something bigger than fish. Stay put unless the red boat tries to leave. Then stop it."

"Don't forget," Sybil told Ralston, "at least one man on that boat is armed."

"Roy here has a gun," Ralston gestured to his security man. "And Stephen, who is with Shelly. Mort has one in the helicopter. We'll call the helicopter to Barateria. I'll have to make sure it arrives *after* we get there, not to scare them away." He called the helicopter, told it to find his boat and trail it to the bayou.

Sybil went aft again with Skipwith: "Still believe your theory?"

"I don't believe it. I see it. It was there all the time. It's marvelous. He had us fighting his enemies, who don't exist. He was uncovering a conspiracy, which doesn't exist. He was rescuing Marcia and Slatkin, from himself. He had us *helping* him, by fighting what he did. All the toys were his, all the pieces on the board. He finally made sense of the world, by making it all over as a game. It's almost a shame to mar such a masterpiece."

"You talk as if you were on his side."

"Part of me always has been, the part I was trying to kill."

"Maybe you'll kill it now."

"I said I had to destroy him. I didn't say I could kill him."

"Are you getting off in New Orleans?"

"No. I'll go to the bayou first. Wingate may be heading there."

Sybil asked the captain if the bayou was reachable by car. "Yes, but by back roads and roundabouts—it would take most of a day to get there." She suggested that Ralston post someone to look for a boat coming behind them with Wingate.

At the cutoff from the Mississippi, the helicopter passed low with a dip, swept on, banked, and hovered far back. Sybil tried to talk with Skipwith but he was unresponsive, wrapped in his thoughts.

The radio again: "Shelly here. There's a helicopter coming down on the landing."

"I told those idiots . . ." Ralston began; then saw his own copter, dangling small in the sky behind them. Skipwith ran forward to the radio. "Land right now! Stop that helicopter from taking off! It's Wingate!"

They had passed a bend just in time to see Shelly's fishing boat dock. They saw people running, too distant to distinguish, and heard a tiny pop that may have been a pistol. Ralston had called up his own copter. It swept past and was landing just as the one on the ground lifted off. "Shall we follow?" the helicopter radioed. Ralston said "Yes."

Skipwith took the radio. "Can you lower a rope to me?"

"A ladder."

"Do." He clambered up onto the pulpit, swaying and slipping.

"Take off your shoes," the captain shouted to him.

"I can't," Skipwith answered as the copter came up over him. "I may need them when we land." He clawed the air as the rope ladder swept by him, then whipped back. He caught the anchor rope with its weighted knot, and risked the trammeling freedom of these bonds. When his climbing foot missed a mesh, the other foot slipped out too, and only his hands held him. He thrashed about with his feet, to pin the live wriggle of ropes, and sudden fear made him want to be lowered again. Only the mocking image of Wingate dispelled the fear. He could not afford fear now, since Wingate was free of it. He relaxed, cooled, not heated, by hatred, caught the ropes between his knees and worked the coils down toward his ankles. He felt as if he were knitting with his shoes, and gave to the operation the kind of childish attentiveness one devotes to meaningless games. It saved his life, for the moment.

When he was almost in the bubble of glass, its pilot moved the bubble forward, making Skipwith feel he was flying himself, horizontal to earth—the pilot shouted, "I've got to move or I'll lose sight of them." The other helicopter had dwindled into the blue smog over New Orleans. Skipwith nodded—he was working too hard to spare any breath for speaking. Mort, the Ralston firm's security man, pulled Skipwith in, grabbing his belt in a way that painfully numbed Skipwith's crotch.

Panting inside, Skipwith felt the throb of rotors speed his heart, and he leaned forward as if his pulse, in turn, would quicken the frail craft's engine. The radio was reconstructing what had happened at the landing. Wingate and two men picked up Marcia—she had been imprisoned in one of the cabins. Wingate left behind Slatkin and the black actor. "He knows I'm the last enemy," Skipwith said to no one.

As the copters did their airy crab-crawl past New Orleans crab houses, Skipwith looked at the jumble of cathedral towers glaring in the white heat, and wondered how he could have forgotten life's cost when he mellowed with the sazerac-glow of cathedral sunsets.

"He may be headed toward Elba," Skipwith said to the other two, and explained what that was and where. His hunch was confirmed before he could finish the explanation. Wingate's copter swept low near the levee and followed its bend toward the Slatkin manor. Skipwith came up just in time to see the landing of the first craft, which kept its rotors turning. Wingate ran for the garçonnière, dragging Marcia.

"Take us down," Skipwith told the pilot, who nodded. The trees were churning like seaweed, from the rotors' power, when the whole copter bucked sideways, its pilot responding to gunfire. Skipwith almost went out the open door, without his ladder this time. The guns fell silent—they wanted to scare this invader off, not bring it down. The pilot swung back out over the river, but Skipwith shouted, "Go over the house and land." His ardor overcame the pilot's delayed buck and rebellion of terror. Mort nodded yes, when the pilot gave him a frightened look.

The copter dangled up over the house and dropped blindly down on a patch of lawn. As soon as the treads rocked level, the pilot tumbled out and lay flat on the ground. Skipwith and Mort imitated him, looking for snipers to appear from the other side of the house. But they saw nothing.

"Cover me," Skipwith told Mort, who had his gun out. Skipwith ran for the house, peered around its corner, then signaled Mort to follow. "They're sticking with the copter, for a quick takeoff."

"Go ahead," said Mort, "I'll cover you again."

"No. Give me the gun. You stay here." There was a mad authority in Skipwith's voice. Mort knew he would have to fight to keep the gun, and he wanted all his enemies on the other side. He handed it over.

Skipwith sprinted for a tree. Those at the copter did not

shoot, but they had leveled their guns. Skipwith fired twice to make them duck, and ran for the garçonnière. He thought it took him an hour to turn the knob and open the door; one bullet hit the door as he got inside it.

The garçonnière was quiet, till he heard a scuffle at the top of the stairs. Wingate's and Marcia's legs came into view at the same time. Wingate had a pouch under his right arm, and a gun in that hand. His left hand steered and jerked Marcia around by the wrist.

Skipwith spoke to Wingate's mild questioning look: "Harris said you were his kind."

"When?"

"Just before he died."

"Chummy scene."

"That wasn't. This is."

"Then move away, chum. I just want a bit of time, then I'll let her go. Do you believe that?"

"Yes," Skipwith answered, but brushed the question away. "He said I was catching it from you. It's time for a cure."

"Killing's the cure? You know better than that."

"What good is knowing it? You set the rules. That's why you can't be allowed to win."

"If I set the rules, at least I play with style."

"The style I could care about . . ."

"If . . ."

"If it left room to care about anything else."

"*This* for a start?" He flung Marcia down on the stair below his, then forced her back to her feet.

"For a start."

"Then make sure she's not your finish, or you hers. Step aside."

He came down another step, Marcia wrestling against him—which made him drop the pouch. He glanced at it, made a mental calculation, and sighed it away. He stepped down again, this time ahead of Marcia, and Skipwith risked a shot on the side away from her. The bullet went wide.

"Bluffing?" Wingate asked, academically. He had not been bluffing, he just missed; but the mere word made him want to retreat into bluster and let Wingate go. He shot again, quickly, as much to keep his resolve up as to stop Wingate. This time he did hit the shin, and wondered inconsequently if it was the same shin Llad had shot.

Wingate half-stumbled. Skipwith saw Marcia wrench herself free and start toward him. "Up!" he shouted. "Go up!" He almost ran up the stairs himself in his eagerness to convey his message. She ran from both men to the landing above.

"Just the two of us," Wingate said, steadying his voice as he hopped down another step on his good leg. His gun had not wavered even when his voice did. Skipwith aimed his own gun, closed his eyes, and resolved to fire at the next sound of that little hop. At this range he could hardly miss.

The gun jumped in his hand when the explosion came, and it took a moment for him to realize he had not blown Wingate's head away. Wingate had. Through a bloody nimbus Skipwith *thought* he saw what he could not see—Wingate's face fall out the back of his head, leaving a cavity-leer in front, a satiric emptiness. The illusion froze Skipwith while Wingate settled to the stairs, on his back, and slithered with puppetlike limbs working independently down toward Skipwith. Skipwith hypnotically watched this death-writhe toward him, till it trammeled him and he fell. When Marcia looked down, they seemed a bloody pair of wrestlers, each trying to shake the other off.

vi

They made nine for breakfast at Brennan's, where Ralston was known for his talent-hunting trips to see Tulane students act and dance. Lewis had brought his wife, and Shelly had brought Joseph and his actor lover. "Comrades in arms," Ralston said, pouring the champagne. "I give you our prize of war, the recaptured Marcia." They drank the toast.

"You have to admit," Skipwith said, "I was right, not wanting to be at Button's in New Orleans."

"I don't know," Ralston said. "Where else could you find a band of friends to match this?"

"You must remember, Wingate was my friend too."

"A friend who had kept you in a limbo removed from life," Sybil said angrily. "At least you have come back to life yourself."

"Except for that part of me I killed."

"I think you can live better without that," Marcia ventured.

"Perhaps."